One Hundred Years from London

A Collection of Short Stories for Light Reading

One Hundred Years from London

A Collection of Short Stories for Light Reading

For information:
The Center for Writing Excellence, a Small Press
Allen, Texas

Email: **janiewrites1@gmail.com**

Website: **http://janiewrites.com**

ISBN-13: 978-0692201770

ISBN-10: 0692201777

Published by: The Center for Writing Excellence

Printed in the United States of America
May 1, 2013; July 12, 2016

Dedication

I dedicate this collection to my Grandchildren:

Patrick	Chloe
Tiana	Ciera
Matthias	Trinity
Darrah	Thane

And to my Great-Grandchildren:

Ciera's Anaiya	Matthias' Amelie
Tiana's Elina	Darrah's Jackson
Patrick's Jace	Ciera's New Baby (due Feb., 2017)

In the fervent hope that they all become avid readers; maybe even writers!

Preface

The first essay in this book, a memoir of my early years, explains a little bit about how I came to be a writer. A story about a cat we once owned follows, and the last essay in this section is a comment on becoming a grandmother, something I never thought would happen.

The fiction stories starting with "What Happened in London: Parts I & II" were written for a variety of reasons. Some are contest entries; some are just because there were stories in my head that I needed to get out onto paper.

The final section of the book contains stories that I wrote together with a friend and fellow writer. I started working with Rhonda when I edited her book, *Ame's Honor* and discovered that we worked well together. We decided to see if we could collaborate on some fiction writing for the NYC Short Fiction and Flash Fiction contests. We had a lot of fun writing those stories, and are now collaborating on a novel based on the first short story we wrote together: *Alexis' Aggravation.*

Table of Contents

Acknowledgements

My family and friends have always supported my writing, and I thank them for that.

The encouragement to continue to hone my craft comes from the many wonderful writers I have met over the years through my website:

The Center for Writing Excellence:
(**http://www.janiewrites.com**)

One Hundred Years from London

A Collection of Short Stories for Light Reading

Personal Essays/Memoir

One Hundred Years from London:
My Early Years

My great-great grandmother, Caroline Elizabeth Jarvis, was born in Burmondsey, Surrey, England, on November 24, 1849. Her parents' names were George Jarvis and Francis Hicks Jarvis. I don't know what her home or life was like then, but what I do know is exactly 100 years later, on Thanksgiving Day, November 24, 1949, in Billings, Montana, USA, I decided to join the family. Great-great Grandmother Caroline and I share the date of our birth, and one day I am going to discover what else we share. For now, though, here is the story of my early years.

My Aunt Edith, Mom's sister, was visiting my parents that Thanksgiving holiday to help when the new baby came. She and Mom prepared the usual Thanksgiving dinner with all the "fixins." Mom had been feeling small twinges in her back all afternoon and figured she was going into labor, but she did not tell anyone. Thanksgiving was her favorite holiday and she knew she would not be given any dinner if she went to the hospital.

She waited until after dinner, just as they started clearing the table, to announce that she was in labor. Dad grabbed her bag, and off they went to the hospital to have me. I arrived at around 7:00 in the evening. How do I know this? Ever since I can remember, I have heard the story about how my Aunt Edith was left alone with my big brother, Roger, who was only 16 months old, and the Thanksgiving dishes. For years after, she would jokingly tell me that I should come and do her Thanksgiving dishes; that I 'owed' her.

Mom told me that when she would take me out in the baby carriage for a walk, everyone would tell her what a beautiful baby I was. Such lovely coloring (I was the prettiest shade of gold, she said). Of course, later she discovered that the reason I was that color was because of jaundice. She said when she looked at me she finally understood why people would say, "My, what a nice...baby," when they saw my big brother as a baby. Roger was bald and his ears stuck out from the side of his head. Mom thought he was beautiful, of course. First baby and all that. However, when I appeared that Thanksgiving she knew what a beautiful baby really looked like - jaundice and all!

About 16 months later, my brother Kelly joined us. The three of us must have been a handful for Mom. Just 16 months apart, all of us in diapers at the same time - and back then there was no such thing as disposable diapers! Our brother, Ricky, did not enter the family until five years later - and by then we three were ready for a new sibling. Although I vaguely remember how furious I was when Mom and Dad came home from the hospital with another boy! I really wanted a sister.

I figured I had another chance four years later when Mom was pregnant again. However, it was not to be - Randy, my fourth brother, was born on February 10, 1960. I was not happy at all! I wanted a sister, but it never happened. As I grew up, though, I began to realize how lucky I was as the only girl in a family of four boys. I always had my own room while my brothers always shared their rooms and I had a bunch of brothers ready to protect and defend me if I needed defending and protecting.

My dad planned a special treat for me on my ninth birthday. Years later in a creative writing class in college, I submitted this story for an assignment on a significant memory from childhood:

My First Date

When I woke this morning, I knew it was a special day. My Dad winked at me over the breakfast table.

"Don't forget, today is your birthday, and I have a very special surprise for you." Dad smiled as he finished his coffee and kissed Mom good-bye. After he left for work, I asked Mom what the surprise was, but she would not say anything.

All day in school I tried to figure out what my Dad could possibly be getting for me that was so special – and so mysterious. I asked Kathy, my best friend, what her Dad got her for her 9th birthday.

"Oh, I got the neatest new bike, and some clothes and junk."

"But I've already got a bike, and I really don't need any new clothes. What could he be getting for me that I need?"

I walked home from school with Kathy, and we parted at the corner. We usually talked for a while, but not today. I just had to get home in a hurry.

"Mom!" I yelled from the front door, "has my present come yet?"

"No, come on in and change your clothes. Help me get this salad ready for dinner." Mom was in the kitchen washing the lettuce. I did not see any sign of a birthday cake, so I figured she had hidden it somewhere to surprise me. I was 9 years old today, almost too old for a birthday cake, but I guessed that Mom would have made one anyway.

"Why don't you answer the door, Janie?" Mom said when the doorbell rang a few minutes later. I dashed to the door, knowing that it was for me.

A boy from the florist shop was standing on the porch with a small box in his hand. I could see a flower through the cellophane top.

"Is Janie Johnston here?"

"Yes, I'm Janie, but why would you be bringing me flowers?"

"Beats me, kid, but that's the name on this card." He handed me the box with a big white envelope addressed to me. I opened up the card, saw Dad's name at the bottom, just below this: "I will pick you up tonight at 6:30. Wear your best dress." The corsage in the box was made of beautiful lavender orchids with tiny white flowers and green lacy ribbons. It was the most beautiful corsage I had ever seen. It might have been the only one I had ever seen, but it was beautiful!

Dad picked me up at 6:30 sharp. He was wearing his new suit, and I wore my pink dress with the white bows. Mom said we made a striking couple. When we got into the car, I asked where we were going.

"Well," Dad was smiling again, "I figured that you were going to grow up pretty soon and start going out with boys, so I decided that your first date should be with the first man in your life. We're going out to dinner, and then dancing."

How exciting! However, he was wrong about boys: I sure was not about to go anywhere with boys, at least not yet.

I did not actually start dating until several years after that, but I will never forget my first date. We went to the Starlight Terrace - a restaurant on the road to the airport. The restaurant is long gone, of course, but the memories of a nine-year old girl on the arm of her dad will never quite go away.

The years between my first date and the time I entered high school are all gone too, lost in snapshots of memory. Girl Scout camp was great fun, I remember. There are three distinct memories that come from that time. My mom was our scout leader and she made sure we had many exciting adventures at Twin Pines Day Camp. We must have been around 10 years old the summer we found "Sheik" the bull snake. He was big and slow. We adopted him and mom taught us how to hold him so he would not be afraid of us.

Some of the other counselors wanted us to be afraid of him, though, and did not think we should be playing with a snake. That was the best summer; we made s'mores, pigs in a blanket, ants on a log, and caramel dumplings. Mom was a great cook, even on a campfire.

One other summer camp memory that stands out is from the first time I went to 'sleep-away' camp. The girls stayed in cabins surrounding the lodge up in the mountains above Red Lodge, Montana. I remember writing home to my parents telling them about my cabin-mates. I even remember their names: Margo Powers, Leslie Harper, and Sonya Martinez. In my letter, I mentioned that one of them was black and one was Mexican, but I did not know which was which. Leslie was the daughter of a dentist and was white. My, I led a sheltered life in Billings in the 50s. We had very little exposure to other cultures in our very white neighborhood and when I ended up in a situation with a black girl and a Mexican girl, I knew they were not white, but other than that could not tell the difference. Even the names did not tell me anything, for all I knew Margo was a Mexican name!

It did not take me long, though, to figure it out. After camp was over that summer, I invited Margo to visit me in my neighborhood. We were riding bikes around when some of the older boys started calling her names that I knew were wrong. We went inside where my mom assured us that the boys were just being mean and they did not know anything. Margo cried and my mom took her home. She never did visit me again.

This brings me to the last real memory I have from my childhood. It was Girl Scout summer camp again, and this time I must have been around 13 or 14. It was CAP camp, or Counselor Apprentice Program, I was in training to be a camp counselor, although I never did become a counselor. I had discovered boys and this turned out to be my last summer as a Girl Scout. The camp was a month long and we stayed in modified covered wagons. We did a lot of things in that camp, learned how to cook over a camp fire, how to lash poles together to make tables, went hiking all over the mountains and thought we were being so wild and independent when we took off our shirts to hike in just our bras because it was so hot.

We camped out under the stars several times, getting our sleeping bags and clothes wet when we got caught in a surprise rain storm. Looking back now at that summer, I marvel at how completely carefree and innocent we were. Of course, we considered ourselves as much more sophisticated and certainly not innocent, but we really were.

In 1966, I started my junior year in high school. I had spent the previous summer terrorizing my parents as a teenager. The one thing that I did, however, that was different was take a summer school class in creative writing. One of my friends, Jackie Vinner, who was a year older than I was and went to school at Billings Senior High, the archrival of Billings West High, where I attended, also took the creative writing class. It was not that we had to take the class, our grades were good and we were not failing any classes, but we wanted to take it.

We spent summer mornings in the classroom while our friends were out doing teenage summer stuff, like hanging around, sleeping, and going to the pool. Jackie and I wrote stories. I do not remember too much about what kind of stories we wrote, but I do remember really liking the class and the opportunity to write.

That fall, my mom talked me into signing up for the Journalism class and I met Mr. Lou Morris, the journalism teacher. Writing for the school paper that year and during my senior year changed my life. For the first time, I felt like a real writer, a feeling that has never changed.

Sir Randall, the Amazing Tuxedo Cat

Sir Randall was an amazing cat. He never saved anyone from a burning building, nor did he trekked across the country in search of his home, but he was still an amazing cat. He was eleven years old when we lost him, and still wore the tuxedo he had on that day eleven years ago when we first saw him in the cage at the animal shelter. The tuxedo was not faded or tattered, it was just as glossy black and brilliantly white as it was on the day we first saw him in the cage with his sister and his mom. That in itself was amazing, but that was not why Sir Randall was amazing.

He had a short tail. Not a bobbed tail and not part of a tail, just a very short tail. It sticks stuck up when he walked, about three inches tall, just stuck up. He sort of waved it as he moved along. We do not know why his tail was so short, his mom and his sister had normal tails, but his was short. That was not why he is amazing, either.

We named him Sir Randall when we got him because he was born on Randy's birthday. Randy was my little brother. He died in a car accident many years before Sir Randall was born. The Sir part came because the little cat was dressed in such a fancy tuxedo. White spats and all. His chest was covered in a bright white, but a bit conservative dress shirt. Not a fussy ruffled shirt, but the kind with embroidered plackets down the front. His jaunty short tail was all black and he had a small white blaze on his face. He was an elegant cat, even when he was a kitten. But that is not why he was amazing.

My granddaughter, Ciera, was six years old that spring, and she picked Sir Randall out. She liked the way he just sat in the cage and blinked at her – as if to say, "I'm an amazing cat, choose me and you will find out why I am amazing." He opened his mouth just a tiny bit, stuck the tip of is tongue out, and just sat there, never taking his eyes off Ciera. His sister, a pretty little grey tabby, bounced around the cage, showing off her long tail while she tried to get Ciera's attention. Ciera ignored her and reached for Sir Randall. He *allowed* her to pick him up and cuddle him in her arms. And that, my cat loving friends, is why he was amazing.

We took him home and from that day on, he and Ciera were fast friends. She would dress him up in her doll clothes, put him in the doll stroller, and drag him around as if he were one of her toys. She carried him all over the house, sometimes just picking him up upside down, his head hanging down and that short tail waving in the air. He did not care. He put up with her as if he knew she would not hurt him, and he simply resigned himself to being her version of a stuffed toy – one that purred. As he got bigger, she stopped dressing him up, but she still dragged him around the house as if he were a stuffed animal. When she watched TV, Sir Randall was her pillow. He would lay there on the floor, not complaining, just waiting for Ciera to move her head so he could escape. He seemed to sigh, as if to say, "Oh my. Here we go again."

When Ciera became a teenager, she rarely had time for her old friend, but that was OK with Sir Randall, because he had a new friend. Ciera's little sister, Trinity, was three years old. From the time she could crawl, she understood that Sir Randall was an amazing cat. And he has understood that here was another little girl who loved him and needed him. Trinity laid on him when she watched TV, just as her big sister did. She tried very hard to pick him up and carry him around, but he is almost as big as she is, and by the time she got him under the front legs and stood up, he was still sitting on the floor. She weighed about 33 pounds, and he weighed at least half that.

Trinity tried to put Sir Randall in her doll stroller, but he was too big. She loved to play in and with boxes and tried to get Sir Randall in the boxes with her. Sometimes she was successful, and he just sat there in the box until she let him go. Sometimes she sat on the floor, holding him under the front legs while he just sat there and let her hold him. He never scratched, or bit. He just sighed, looked at me with those liquid eyes of his as if to say, "Oh my, here we go again." Then he would go limp in her arms, purr contentedly, and wait. When she did let him go, he walked a few steps away, then lay down. He was, after all, nine years old and has lived a long life for a cat. Sometimes he hid under the bed in my room, but when Trinity found him, he came out and *allowed* himself to be cuddled, carried, and dragged around. Just as if he were a big stuffed toy.

Sir Randall was the most mellow, amazing cat I have ever had the pleasure of being around. He allowed all his cat friends to come in the house through his kitty door, watched as they ate his food, and watched again as they sauntered out through the kitty door onto the patio. Then he would talk my daughter, Ciera and Trinity's mother, into putting more food into his bowl. The one and only time he got into a fight, he was injured quite badly and we had to take him to the vet. He got 27 stitches in his side and had to wear a lampshade to keep him from biting out the stitches. The fur over the scar originally grew in white and we thought for sure his tuxedo would forever look as though it was torn. The black grew back in though, and we could not see where the scar was.

All our friends were amazed at how amazing Sir Randall was. They laughed when they see him sitting on his backside in the big chair in the living room, his hind legs splayed out, his front paws folded on his chest and his glorious white dress shirt spotless. He often sat that way right next to Trinity, both in the same chair, both limp as rag dolls while they watched TV.

Sir Randall did not run when he saw Trinity heading for him, he just relaxed. Trinity ran when she saw him, though. No matter what she was doing, if he walked across the room and caught her eye, she dropped whatever she was doing, and ran to try and pick him up. "Kitty!" she cried as she reached for him. He stopped, flopped down on the floor, and waited for the inevitable. He did not try to get away. He just lay there and **allowed** Trinity to love him because he loved her, too.

He was truly amazing and we continue to miss him every day!

Slow Motion Moments

Being a grandmother was never part of my life plan. I always knew I would have children, in fact I started pretty early with my first baby at 18. I never did think about being a grandmother, I was so busy taking care of that first tiny boy, who was followed by two sisters in the next five years. There were diapers to change, first steps to monitor, and school assignments to help with. It was a busy time, with no time for thinking about being a grandmother. Being a mother was hard enough.

Now, when I think about it, I am sure my children are still out playing in the back yard – aren't they? They were the last time I checked. At least that is how I remember it. When did they grow up? How is it that my son, who was so tiny when he was born six weeks early, talks about HIS 6'2" son taking classes to become a chef? And my daughter, who I am sure just graduated from 8th grade, called the other day to tell me about HER daughter graduating from college with a BS in nursing!

Oh, there is my youngest daughter. She isn't any older than six is she? Why just last week she fell out of the back of a slow moving pickup and has a couple of black eyes to show for it! She is always doing something like that. Wait, who is that with her? Her daughter AND granddaughter? When did that happen?

My son told me one day that I needed to take 'grandma lessons' from my mother. I told him that was a silly notion. My mother spent her grandmother years knitting, baking cookies, and taking care of my dad. They retired and moved to the southwest. She knew how to be a grandmother, I did not have the faintest idea how I would do that. I had a business to run, classes to teach, and writing to do. I did not have time for 'grandma lessons' but more importantly, I did not need lessons on how to be a grandma because I did not plan on ever being a grandmother!

Mom passed away several years ago and dad moved into an assisted living facility for his final years. I could not take 'grandma lessons' now if I wanted to. It would be a good idea now, though, because I am a grandmother. I have eight beautiful grandchildren – the newest one a little, tiny, preemie boy born just three weeks ago to my youngest daughter who is also a grandmother! Her little son is 10 weeks younger than his niece.

It all happened so fast, yet there are parts of the past years that seemed to move in slow motion. The day my daughter fell out of the truck is one of those slow motion days. It took forever get out of the pickup, get to the back of it, pick her up, and race to the hospital. Afterward I remember thinking that I knew what it felt like to run in slow motion. The next thing I knew I was holding her hand as she gave birth to her daughter. It seemed like only weeks later when that little baby girl became a mother herself.

Another time I drove 600 miles across Montana to pick my son up where he was living with his father and stepmother. He had been there a little over two years when he called me and begged me to come and get him. Those 600 miles were the longest 600 miles I ever travelled. It felt like I was driving backward it took so long to get to him. I blinked and he was calling me from his home in Germany to tell me about the new company he was starting. His three children are all out of school now and starting their own lives. His biggest desire is to become a grandfather. I never expected to be a grandmother, and my son wants grandchildren so bad he said if his kids didn't get busy he was going to adopt some! He may have to do that. His children are involved with creating careers, not grandchildren for him, at least not yet.

Then there was the day my middle child walked across the stage at the high school in her beautiful gown to be crowned runner-up in the Miss Teen Montana pageant. That was a slow motion day, she was lovely and smiling shyly as her father escorted her. She played the saxophone for her musical number while dressed in a white top hat, white tails, and white satin shorts. The next thing I knew, they wheeled my daughter into the operating room to remove a grapefruit sized benign tumor from her brain as I was holding her six-year old daughter. Fourteen long hours later, the doctors said she was going to be just fine. This spring I attended the graduation of that six year old as she received her BS in nursing and is now preparing for a career as a nurse. Her mom is rightly very proud of her. *(Update, that once little girl is going to be a mom herself this fall.)*

I remember the bright yellow kitchen in the first house we bought when the kids were little. I would close the curtains in that kitchen window because the swing set was in the backyard and it made me nervous to watch the kids climbing on it. I probably should have left it open so I could see them more clearly as they grew. If I close my eyes now I still imagine their small, shadowy shapes on the other side of those thin curtains. Maybe if I had left the curtains open I would have seen that they were growing up and preparing to move into their own lives.

So, yes, I am a grandmother, and even a great-grandmother! It is amazing when I think about it. It took what seemed like minutes, not years, to get here. Those years passed by in a blur, with slow motion moments shining through.

(UPDATE: Six years after the original writing of this story, my son has two granddaughters and one grandson.)

General Fiction

I started out writing non-fiction. All my early schooling is in the art of reporting and article writing; however, I discovered a love for fiction when I decided to write a story for a contest honoring Agatha Christie – a mystery writer. The story "Tumbleweeds" in the *All About Families* section came from that first venture into fiction writing.

What Happened in London . . .

Part I: Spelling Murder

"Don't you worry, Freddie, they'll not win!" Marie whispered, nodding her head toward the crowd.

"Who'll not win? God's eyes, Marie, they're about to hang us!" Frederick's panic-stricken face sunk even lower, fear taking control of his limbs as he sagged under the arms of the guards.

"Maybe so, but they won't win! I've seen to that! I'll be back. If it takes a hundred years, I'll be back!"

"Yer daft, woman!" Indignation puffed Frederick up; seeing the ropes swinging in front of him made him sag back down.

People usually kept behind closed doors that winter to avoid the misery created by mud and incessant rain along with fear of a cholera outbreak that had already claimed 53,000 lives. However, on November 13, 1849, the crowd in front of the Horsemonger Lane Gaol, Bermondsey District, South London, swelled, jeering and hissing as the accused started up the gallows stairs in the pouring rain.

Frederick did not object as the hangman dropped a dirty cloth bag over his eyes, but Marie threw hers off with a toss of her head. After glaring at the hangman, she screamed out to the crowd, "Just wait! I'll be back!"

For several months before the hanging, the Mannings had been having financial problems. In one of many attempts to reverse their fortunes, Frederick took a job at a pub, Old King John's Head, near the Goding Brewery on Old Kingsland Road. When Frederick tried to set up an account at Goding Brewery to furnish ale to the pub, his ruined credibility forced the Brewery to require the surrender of local scrip and bearer securities as collateral.

An infuriated Marie tried in vain to get the securities returned. She became desperate when Frederick, accused of pilfering from the cash drawer, lost his post at the pub. About this time, Marie discovered a group of people exploring the world of black magic under Madame Blavatsky's leadership.

This Secret Society turned out to be just what Marie was looking for. She defended Blavatsky, claiming that she, too, had occult powers. "Just think; I can use my magical powers to conjure up money!"

Although Frederick was skeptical, he did not argue with her. Instead, he brought up his own moneymaking idea. "Marie, do you ever see your old friend, Patrick O'Conner?" he asked, knowing that Marie had been carrying on with O'Conner behind his back for over a year.

"What?" Her voice sharp, eyes wary, she turned toward Frederick. "Whatever are you talking about?" Marie dropped Blavatsky's black magic book, trying to discern just how much Frederick knew about her relationship with O'Conner.

"I heard he was loaded." Frederick continued, ignoring Marie's thinly disguised anxiety. "Maybe we could borrow some cash from him, since you two are old friends."

"Well now, that might just be an idea." Marie mused, thinking she could ply O'Conner with black magic and maybe even pull a double-cross on Frederick, getting more money and hiding some of it. "I will invite him over to dinner next week."

The next day, Marie met with Madame Blavatsky. "What I really need, Helena, is a spell for money. I don't care what kind of magic, I just need money and I need it quickly!" Marie was more agitated than usual, first rubbing her hands together, then on her skirt, then pulling them through her hair, all while pacing back and forth in Blavatsky's foyer.

"Why is it so urgent that you get money?" Helena asked, watching Marie's nervous pacing with a slightly bored expression. "Really, Marie, it can't be as bad as all that can it?"

"Oh, aye, it can be." Marie stopped pacing and pulled a sheaf of papers out of her bag, shaking them. "Frederick gambled away all our savings. Now we've got these payments due!"

"Well, I know a few spells to get you money, but the key to them working properly is to know someone who will give you money – with magical help, of course."

"Oh," Marie stopped pacing, "I know someone with a lot of money all right, but he hangs onto it like it's going to disappear. I don't think he will just hand it over. That's why I need the spell; to make him give it up."

"I know just what you need." Helena disappeared, leaving Marie in the foyer staring after her. A bright flash followed by a loud thunderclap briefly lit up the sky and rain blew in through the still open front door.

Marie pushed the door shut against the wind. "Helena! Where did you go? The foyer is all wet!"

"Here I am." Helena appeared behind Marie, startling her. "Oh! Careful, don't spill it!" She was holding a gold chalice filled with a dark red liquid.

"Ohhhh, is that, uh…blood?" Marie asked, peering at the chalice.

"Oh, don't be so dramatic!" Helena scolded her. "It's red wine – just what we need for the spell. This will guarantee your friend will hand over his money when you ask." Grinning, she placed the chalice on a spindly table near a side chair. "Now, come over here and sit down."

"Place your hands thus over the chalice." Helena stacked her open hands over the wine, and then moved away so Marie could imitate her.

"Say these words:

"Money is powerful,
Money is mine.
Money for me,
None for thee.
Money will be all mine.
Money is everywhere.
Now make me take it from there."

"Memorize them. Stack your hands over the wine while saying them. After your friend drinks the wine, ask him for money and he will give it to you."

Patrick O'Conner came to dinner at the Manning home on Thursday, August 9. The invitation, coming the week before, was a surprise; he was nervous about being in the same room with both the Mannings. He was not sure how much Frederick knew of his relationship with Marie, but he also was not one to turn down a free meal.

Moments before Patrick's arrival, Frederick observed Marie mumbling something as she held her hands over a goblet of wine. "What are you up to now?"

"Nothing, just a bit of foolishness Helena told me about. Supposed to bring luck to whoever drinks the wine. Silly, I know." Marie knew Frederick did not approve of her new fascination with magic.

"Well, I suppose conjuring up a bit of luck isn't a bad thing." Frederick sighed. "But enough of that nonsense now. I hear O'Conner coming through the gate."

Marie nodded, placing the goblet near the guest place setting and adding a similar goblet to both hers and Frederick's places.

"Hello, Marie." O'Conner said somewhat nervously upon his entry into the kitchen. "Thank you for inviting me to join you both for dinner." He looked at Frederick, who also seemed a bit nervous.

"Actually, Patrick, this is more of a business meeting than a social call." Frederick licked his lips, picked up his goblet and took a nervous sip. "Um, Marie and I were wondering ..."

"Let the man sit down and relax a minute before you start in with business." Marie reprimanded her husband. "Do take a drink of your wine and let's have our meal first." She added, looking at O'Conner and smiling, gesturing toward the goblet of wine.

The three ate in companionable silence for a few minutes, and then Frederick tried again. Clearing his throat, he stated, "We would like to discuss a business proposition with you, Patrick."

"What sort of business?" O'Conner was wary now, wondering just what Manning meant.

"A loan. We'll pay it back, of course, but, you see, um, well, we know you lend money and were wondering if you would help us out."

"I usually conduct business during business hours, not social encounters. I don't have any money with me and even if I did, I wouldn't loan it to you. Loaning money to friends never works out." O'Conner dismissed the request and went back to his meal.

"What?" An enraged Marie got up abruptly, grabbed Patrick's goblet, turned her back on the men, mumbled something, poured more wine in the goblet, nearly spilling it when she slammed it back down in front of Patrick. "Try the wine again!"

Patrick knocked over the goblet and stood up at Marie's frightful behavior. "I'm leaving now."

Marie grabbed a shovel from behind the door, and struck O'Conner over the head with it, knocking him unconscious. Frederick, horrified at what Marie had done, stood up. Marie shouted, "He was supposed to give us the money! The spell didn't work!"

"What're we going to do now?" Frederick asked, "When he wakes he is likely to murder us!"

"Not if we kill him first!

Eight days later, both Mannings were in the Horsemonger Lane Gaol, accused of murder. They were hanged on November 13, 1849.

One hundred years later, on November 13, 1949, a woman dreamed of rain, mud, and crowds of jeering people just before giving birth to a little girl in rural Montana.

Part II: Twila Turns 18

Twila opened her eyes slowly, bringing the room into a fuzzy kind of focus. She felt more than saw the sheer curtains stir in the early morning light, the window partially open to the brisk November air. She lay on the bed, her legs tangled in the sheets and sighed before turning her head to squint at the alarm clock.

"7:15. I guess that's better than waking at 4:00 and lying here waiting for the sun to come up." She thought, vaguely remembering the dream that was even now scattering into smoky tendrils slowly seeping out of her thoughts. Something about, what was it? *"Scaffolding, lots of people. A party, or maybe just a crowd. Can't remember. Oh well. Just another weird birthday dream."* Twila untangled her legs, scooted them over the edge of the bed, and sat up. She had an odd familiar feeling; something right at the edge of her consciousness trying to poke into her now awake mind.

Today was November 13, 1967, Twila's 18th birthday. For as long as she could remember, Twila woke on her birthday feeling out of sorts. Sometimes she woke from dreams like the one that drifted out of her reach this morning, and sometimes she woke in a cold sweat, sure someone was about to hurt her in some way. The feeling did not last, but every year she remembered too late that waking on her birthday was never fun. At least today, the sun, weak as it was in November, was shining.

Twila grinned to herself, banished the dream fragments permanently, and stretched before she hopped off the bed and headed for the bathroom down the hall. Her sister, Imogene, had not gotten up yet. Imogene was 17 and Twila just three when their mother disappeared from their 'wrong side of the tracks' shanty home in the small Western Montana town near the Golden Sunlight Mine. The girls had different fathers, which accounted for the fact that they did not look much alike. Imogene's father died when she was ten. Her mother told her he was coming home from a bar and hit a deer going 90 miles an hour. He was drunk. Neither he nor the deer survived.

Imogene told Twila that her dad was a transient miner, attracted by the gold mine, but put off by the harsh Montana winter. He left about a month before Twila was born. The two girls had been on their own for fifteen years; eventually moving into a nicer apartment just on the 'better' side of the tracks.

Raising Twila was not hard. She was a sunny, happy child, even during the months after her mother disappeared. She talked about her sometimes, but Imogene had pretty much raised her even before their mom left. Twila naturally gravitated toward Imogene who doted on her little sister. The only problems the girls seemed to have revolved around Twila's birthday every year.

Sometimes during the days leading up to her birthday Twila became moody or preoccupied. On the day of her birthday, she often woke screaming and crying from bad nightmares. Sometimes the nightmares came in the middle of the night, leaving Twila exhausted in the morning. There were a few years when they were not so bad, especially when Twila was younger. They did seem to be getting worse as Twila got older, but she was learning to cope with them better and did not seem to be as affected by them.

This year Twila was determined to have a great birthday, despite the dreams. She quickly shrugged off the mood threatening to spoil her day and happily went to wake her sister.

"Hey! Imogene!" Twila shouted as she hurried down the hallway. "Time to get up! Today is my birthday and the sun is actually shining! It's going to be a good day!"

Wrong Number

"Hold on! I'm coming!" Heath heard the cell phone ringing as he was trying to get his key in the door while balancing the pizza box from the take-out deli downstairs, his laptop case, and the extra-large soda he knew he should have not bought.

"Wait a minute! My cell phone is in my pocket – and it is not ringing," he thought as the soda tipped off the pizza box and splatted on the entryway floor. He slowly pushed the door open, looking around to see who was in his apartment with a ringing cell phone. No one was there and the ringing stopped.

"Must have been the neighbor's phone," He mumbled as he stepped over the puddle of soda slowly spreading into the hallway. The pizza box and laptop case landed on the coffee table as he headed through the living room to the kitchen for a wad of paper towels. The cell phone started ringing again, stopping Heath in his tracks. He turned toward the counter in what seemed like slow motion, staring at the unfamiliar phone vibrating and ringing next to the flour canister.

"Heh, heh, hello?" The phone was one of the flip varieties and it took a few seconds for Heath to open it because his hands were shaking. At first, there was no answering sound in the phone but just as Heath took it away from his ear to look at it; he heard a voice whine, "Why didn't you answer before? I've been calling for hours!"

"Uh, I, uh, I just got here. Who is this and whose phone is this?" Heath tore several sheets off the paper towel roll while he cradled the phone between his head and shoulder. He walked over to the doorway and the spilled soda. As he bent down to wipe up the sticky mess, a pair of tennis shoes stepped into his line of site next to the puddle. His gaze travelled up, noticing the jeans covered legs, the frayed bottom of a red jersey all the way to a hard, frowning face topped off with a shiny bald head. "And who are you?" he said as he straightened up.

"I think that call is for me," the stranger said, reaching for the phone still pinned to Heath's shoulder by his ear. Heath wordlessly handed the phone over, then just stood there staring as the stranger turned away and carried on a hurried and hushed conversation with the caller, then pocketed the phone. He gave Heath a quick glance, and then turned as if to leave. "Wait!" Heath called, "What is going on here?"

"Wrong number," the stranger said as he started down the stairs.

"What do you mean wrong number? Why was that phone in my apartment?" Heath followed the bald man, peppering him with questions and getting no response. The bald stranger turned around the corner at the bottom of the steps and was gone by the time Heath got there. He stared at the empty street a minute, then trudged slowly back up the stairs.

Although he was still puzzling over the events the night before, Heath got up and prepared to go to work in the morning. In fact, by the middle of the next week, he had almost forgotten about it. Nothing strange happened again and Heath went about his days, everything the same as the day before. That is, the same until about 10 days after the strange incident with the phone, when he was ordering a take-out pizza from the deli below his apartment. The deli owner also owned the apartments upstairs and he was working the counter when the door to the deli opened and the bald man walked in.

"It's you!" Heath exclaimed, "Who are you and why was your phone in my apartment 10 days ago?" The man behind the counter looked from Heath to the bald man, clearly confused. "Uh, Mr. Hildago said he was your brother-in-law, married to your sister. I let him in your apartment. He said he talked to you and you were going to leave a key under the mat for him, but must have forgotten."

"I don't have a sister." Heath said, enunciating each word carefully as he glared at his landlord. "I'm calling the police!"

"No, don't do that." Hildago was unusually calm. "I can explain"

"Then start explaining. You have five minutes before I call the cops." Heath moved toward Hildago, waving his finger (which was shaking slightly) in his face. "And it better be good!"

Hidalgo's story shocked Heath and he was having a hard time believing that Hildago had been spending almost every day for the past two months in his apartment! There was never any evidence of anyone being there, except for the one time he forgot and left his phone on the counter.

"You can't just camp out in someone else's apartment during the day when they are at work!" Heath was sitting at one of the round tables in the deli, Hildago across from him.

"But I didn't touch your things; I just needed a place to set up my surveillance camera so I could watch the building across the street. It was a top-secret mission and nobody could know or my cover would be blown! I did not know who I could trust because I did not know if either of you were involved."

"So what about your cover now?" the landlord asked.

"That is why I am here today, we arrested the people we were watching last night. There is no more need for our surveillance operation. I came to return the key I took off your spare key ring the first day I was in your apartment and explain what I was doing." He dropped the key on the table and walked out, leaving Heath and the landlord staring after him.

Writing Contest

The short story contest was just about to start, and Evie anxiously watched her email account, waiting for prompt. She just knew she would win this time! She had entered the contest every time it ran, but always came in somewhere past 5th place. There were only prizes awarded to the first five places. She had spent the entire weekend thinking of clever phrases and practicing literary devices that she was sure she could use in the story, no matter what the prompt was. The email was supposed to come out at 9:45 AM. Evie had been staring at her computer screen for the past 20 minutes, willing her email program to beep, telling her she had a new message. It was still only 9:40 AM. Five minutes to go.

She jumped when the doorbell rang. "Not now!" she groaned, pushing back her chair and edging toward the door with her eyes still on her screen. She had a whole week to write the story, but was so anxious to start; she did not want to miss a minute of that week answering the door!

When she opened the door, forced to look away from her computer screen, all thoughts of writing fled from her mind. The uniformed man at the door held out a large, flat envelope, splashed with the logo from an express delivery company. Evie saw her hand, shaking like a leaf, automatically reach for the envelope. When her fingertips touched the envelope, she jerked her hand back as if it had been burned.

"Lady," The delivery driver sounded bored. "I need you to sign here for this envelope."

"Um, oh, um." Evie fumbled for the dangling stylus to sign the electronic pad the driver was holding. She hurriedly scratched something on the worn pad and, somewhat reluctantly, reached again for the envelope, without looking directly at it. "Thank-you," she mumbled to the back of the driver as he headed for the white and green truck idling on the street, ignoring her.

Evie leaned against the door jam, staring at nothing as the envelope slipped from her hand. Her heart was beating so loud in her ears that she didn't hear the car enter the driveway. It was only when the door slammed that she slowly turned her head toward the sound.

"Did it come?" Jeremy, Evie's twin brother, practically leaped up the steps onto the porch and snatched up the envelope at Evie's feet. 'I told you it would be here today!" Jeremy crowed as he ripped open the envelope and took out a sheaf of paper stapled to a photo. The twins had not seen their father for years, but Jeremy had found him in an online search. The grainy photo, obviously taken from a high angle, showed their long lost father pointing a gun at their mother, two small children cowering next to her.

Evie turned wordlessly from the door and walked woodenly to her desk. On the screen, an email message flashed. She opened it and stared at the prompt for the fiction contest:

Use this as your starting sentence:

"If I could do one day over in my life, it would be...."

The Garnet Ring

"Howdy." Dale nodded to the young man leaning out the window, his hair, along with the rest of him, in need of a wash. "Need some gas?"

"Um, well, yeah." The man said, "How much can I get for a dollar?"

He twisted the broad gold band of a ring on his right hand, briefly exposing a large, square garnet.

"That'd be 'bout five gallons, I 'spect." Dale started toward the pump.

"Wait!" Will you take this ring in exchange for the gas? I think it's worth a couple dollars at least. I can bring your dollar in later today, but I'm out of gas now."

"I don't know. The boss doesn't like me to trade stuff." Dale said, nervously scratching the top of his head, cap held out by a couple fingers. "Let me see it."

The man twisted the ring a couple more times, then pulled it off and handed it to Dale. The garnet was square and flat, about a half-inch across. The gold band looked new. "OK, but you have to promise me you will be back to pick this up today."

"I will be here. It's my daddy's ring and I need to give it back to him."

Dale put the ring in his pocket, pulled the nozzle out of the pump, stuck it into the gas tank, and squeezed the handle, watching the numbers turn on the pump.

"There you go," he said as he re-holstered the gas nozzle. "Be sure to be back here before 7:00 when we close."

"Thanks! I'll be here." The man waved his arm out the window as he drove off, kicking up the dust again behind the old truck, one wide fender shaking a bit where the bolts were missing.

A couple more customers broke up the boredom of the afternoon, one family with three noisy kids in the backseat of their sedan. They waved to him through the long, narrow oval window in the back as they drove away. The other customer just bought a coke and stood around drinking it.

"Here's a nickel for the coke, but I don't have the two pennies for the deposit." He said as he finished it and handed the empty bottle and the nickel to Dale.

Dale nodded, took the empty bottle and the nickel, and looked down the street for about the hundredth time in the past half hour. The old pickup was not anywhere to be seen.

At seven o'clock, Dale, after one more look down the street, pulled a dollar bill out of his pocket, shook his head, put it into the cash register and slid the ring on his right hand ring finger. It fit perfectly.

That night at dinner, Dale's dad commented on the ring, wondering aloud where he got it.

"I've seen a ring like that before." He said, "One of the guys usta be on my work crew wore it."

"How come he's not on your work crew any longer?" Dale twisted the ring, looked at the square, red stone, then picked up his fork.

"Oh, he retired a while ago. But I remember when he took that ring off after getting it caught in the handle of one of the trashcans. 'Bout took his finger off when he swung the can up to dump it. Said he gave it to his son."

"That must have been his son who came into the station today. Left it for me to hold for a dollar's worth of gas. Soon's he comes back with my dollar, I'll give him back his ring."

Days, then weeks passed and the man never did come back to the Texaco station to retrieve the ring. Dale wore it every day, and soon it became a part of his daily routine; he felt something was missing if he took it off.

Dale's dad kept asking what branch of the service he was going to enlist in, and his mom kept telling him he did not need to make a decision right now. He already had a couple brothers in the military and she was not anxious about another son joining up.

One day, about two months after the man left the garnet ring with Dale, a car drove up under the breezeway roof that extended out from the front of the service station to cover the pumps. It looked to Dale like it was a brand new 1940 Ford. There were two men in the car, both in Army uniforms. They were laughing about something, not paying much attention to Dale as he walked out to the car, wiping his greasy hands on a red shop rag.

"What can I do for you fellas?"

"Well, I guess you can put some gas in this brand new car. That is what you do here, isn't it? Put gas in cars?" The driver laughed, and poked his friend, indicating Dale with his other hand. "What a dufus!" He said, as if Dale couldn't hear him. "Must be why he is not in the service, the Army don't take dummies!"

Dale just shook his head and started pumping the gas. He had run across this type before: guys all puffed up with their own importance. "That'll be $2.00 for the gas," he said while sliding the nozzle back into the slot at the side of the pump.

"Sure, cracker! Here's your $2.00!" The driver flung the bills out the window at Dale, laughed, and hit the gas pedal, flinging dust up behind him as he roared out of the station.

After twisting the garnet ring around his finger, Dale stooped down and picked up the money. He wiped the dust off the bills and headed back into the station to put them into the cash box.

That night at dinner, while watching his mom dishing up the potatoes, Dale told his dad he had made a decision about enlisting. His dad, a Marine veteran from the first war, waited patiently for his son to provide more information. His mom stopped spooning potatoes from the pan into the bowl on the table.

"I am going to go see the recruiter tomorrow down at the court house."

"Ok, son. You do what you have to do."

Dale's mom, her eyes averted, started to scoop the potatoes out of the pan again. Her shoulders slumped as she turned back to the stove; she stood there for a minute before turning back to Dale.

"Son, are you sure? You know you don't have to go. You already have two brothers over there."

"Yes, mom, I do have to do this. It's time." Dale stood up, walked over and gave his mom a kiss, then left the room. "I'm not hungry right now. I will get something later." He subconsciously twisted the garnet ring on his right hand.

One month later, as he was leaving the house for the last time before going to Navy boot camp, he handed the ring to his dad. "Will you take care of this for me? I don't want to take a chance on losing it ... uh, over there."

On June 4, 1942, two years after Dale enlisted in the Navy, he was on board the USS Enterprise when the Japanese attacked it during the Battle of Midway. The ship was dead in the water, having sustained heavy damage, and several of Dales' crewmates were killed.

Dale, shrapnel wounds on his right hand and arm, was sent home to recover. Because of the swelling, he could not wear the garnet ring, although his dad tried to give it back to him. "No, Dad, you hang onto it. I don't want it lost and I can't wear it."

His dad wore the garnet ring until he passed in 1975, when Dale finally took it back. He had regained most of the use of his hand over the years, and when he put the ring back on, he told his son it felt right, finally.

When Dale passed in 2012, the ring went to his son, who wears it to this day.

Western Fiction

Someone once encouraged me to write a story set in the old West – a part of the country I grew up in an lived in, but had never written about. The Duplicate Saloon is a flight of fancy set in the old West. I'm not sure where it came from, but here it is . . .

The Duplicate Saloon

Doc pushed his hat back on his head, leaving a streak of dust rimming his forehead just above washed-out grey eyes. The dust clogged in the creases outside each eye as he squinted in the bright Arizona sun. His horse shuffled his feet across the desert floor, head down, eyes nearly closed. He did not even notice the lizard that crossed in front of them, stopping to flick its tongue and blink at the drooping rider above the plodding horse.

"Well, Sundance, I kin just barely see the shacks outside Dry Gulch now. We should be in town soon. I surely do hope the saloon has lots o' whiskey. I'm right parched." Doc's dry tongue scraped across even drier lips. The horse did not respond.

On the other side of town, on the roof above the general store, Snake-Eye Jackson squinted into the desert, too. Only he was looking at the speck moving toward town on the horizon. The speck slowly turned into the figure of a man on a horse, and a tired, drooping man and horse at that. "Humpf! I don' 'spect Bullet is dumb enough to just ride into town like that, brazen as can be." Snake-Eye mused to himself as he watched the weary rider approach. "I heard he was on his way to Dry Gulch, but that cain't be him!"

Snake-Eye had been hiding on the roof most of the day, hoping to get a glimpse of Bullet Richards, orneriest, meanest sum-bitch in the southwest, before anyone else saw him. Snake-Eye wanted to kill Bullet and get away from town before anyone even knew he was there. His gut still burned as he thought about that poker game in Lone Tree, up in Colorado Territory, a couple months ago. The two of them had plotted to cheat their way to winning a big stake in the game, but Bullet snuck out of town right after the game and took all the money with him. Snake-Eye had been hunting for him ever since.

"Well, I'll be horn-swaggled! If it ain't Doc Henderson!" Snake-Eye's one good eye widened as the lone rider got close enough he could see the dusty beard trailing down the front of Doc's sun-faded vest. That beard could only belong to Doc. It was his one pride-and-glory. "I wonder what that old hired gun is doing here, of all places?" Snake-Eye scrambled back from the edge of the roof as he saw Doc push his hat back on his head and all but look him in the eye.

"Stop pickin' yer teeth, Angie!" the barkeep yelled over at the chunky, garishly dressed barfly while he lazily swiped a dirty rag over an even dirtier bar. "It's getting' so even the oldest, drunkest, and ugliest cowboy don't even want to come near the bar with you standin' there!"

"Oh, shut up, Duke!" Angie brushed the dried out straw-like hair off her face and struck a pose at the end of the bar. "There was a day when the cowboys used to fight over me! Why, I remember these two…"

"Aw, Angie, them days is long gone. You might jest as well fergit about them. Those two old gunfighters are prolly dead by now. You sure as shoot ain't never gonna see neither one o' them agin!" Duke finished washing the bar and threw his rag at Angie. "Now, git off that there bar stool, git yerself cleaned up, and help me get set up fer the evenin' rush!"

"What evenin' rush? Why, there ain't been but two-three old drunks in here in weeks . . ." Angie's voice trailed off as the swinging doors whooshed open, leaving a man's silhouette against the setting desert sun in the open doorway. She stared at the man as he slowly moved toward the bar. His face was shielded by his hat, but that beard – there was something familiar – "Oh my gosh!" Angie breathed, could it be? She sat back down heavily on the bar stool, stealing a glance at her face in the cloudy mirror.

"Howdy, stranger!" Buck grinned at the newcomer, hoping to encourage him to buy something. "Can I get you something to wet yer throat?

"Yeah, whiskey, and leave the bottle." The stranger tossed a silver dollar on the bar as he turned to look at Angie, who was desperately trying to fix her appearance in the old mirror. "Angie, is that you? Why, I'll be! Ain't never figured to see you agin!"

Out behind the corral next to the livery stable, a shadow moved in the approaching desert night. The horses in the corral whinnied softly as they detected something moving along the fence line. The shadow paused, and crouched lower as the horses stirred restlessly. "Whoa, fellas. It's OK now." A soft voice floated out over the corral, steadying the horses. The shadow grew taller, stretching to the height of a man, one with a pair of saddlebags flung over his shoulder. He slipped over the fence, and, keeping the bodies of the horses between him and the light from a solitary lantern in the livery stable, moved through the herd, softly reassuring them as he went.

Bullet Richards had arrived, on foot, in Dry Gulch. He snuck into the stable, found an empty stall, slunk inside the partially open door and buried the saddlebags under the straw spread on the floor. He crouched there for a few minutes, listening for sounds of anyone else in the area. After a while, he decided there was nobody about, so he lay down, pulled his hat over his face, and went to sleep.

Snake-Eye moved across the general store roof, climbed down the back of the building using the boxes he had stacked up earlier as steps, and jumped the last few feet to the dirt track running behind the store. He brushed off his pants, squared his hat on his head, and stepped out into the street in front of the store as if he belonged there. "Guess if Bullet is coming to town he must be planning to sneak in under cover of darkness." Snake-Eye mumbled. "Howdy, ma'am." H tipped his hat to a woman who eyed him suspiciously as she passed by. "Nice evenin' ain't it?" She nodded, stepped around him, and went on, looking back once with no comment.

Snake-Eye continued toward the saloon, noting the fading sign above the swinging doors: The Duplicate Saloon: Double Yer Fun. "Ha, I just bet!" he snickered. "What kind of fun could be had in this worn-out town?" He pushed the swinging doors aside and looked in. All he saw in the gloom was some old cowboy, his back to the door, over at the end of the bar talking to a worn-out hussy, who seemed to be preening herself, although he could not figure out why. The barkeep was watching the pair with a somewhat bored smile on his face.

"Hey! Barkeep! How about a drink?" Snake-Eye stepped up to the bar and slapped a half-dollar down. Duke poured a glass of whiskey and set it down on the bar next to the coin. "You want some change, or are you going to have another?" He asked, eyeing the coin as if it were going to disappear. "Leave it, I might want another." Snake-Eye growled. He was still not happy about not finding Bullet.

Both the cowboy and the hussy turned at the sound of his voice, and both of them stared at Snake-Eye. The cowboy with distaste, and the hussy with amazement. "Snake-Eye." They said at the same time.

"Yeah, Doc, I figured that was you. I saw you ride into town from the north. But, who the hell are ...?" Snake-Eye's one eye widened for the second time that day. "Angie, as I live and breathe!"

It took a few minutes for everyone to recover their surprise at seeing each other again. The last time these three were together was on a riverboat out of St. Louis. Angie was one of the hostesses and Doc and Snake-Eye were playing poker. Both the gun fighters were enraptured by Angie, who was young, slender, and pretty. The three of them had a high old time on that riverboat trip, but it all ended when Angie declared she could not go with either of them when the trip was over. She did not want to give up her life as a riverboat princess to go live in the Wild West with one of the gun slinging gamblers.

In the years since that river trip, the gun fighters went their separate ways out West, with Doc hiring himself out to find and bring in bank robbers for small towns in Montana and Wyoming Territories who could not afford to hire a full time sheriff. Snake-Eye continued to gamble his way through Colorado, Utah and now in to Arizona Territory, staying just barely on the wrong side of the law. Angie's fortunes steadily decreased until she found herself working in this tiny, desolate bar in Dry Gulch, Arizona.

"So, why are you here, Doc?" Snake-Eye wanted to know. "I thought I heard you were working for the law in Montana and Wyoming."

"I am. I was hired by the town of Deadwood, Wyoming to bring in a notorious bank robber who hit the bank there." Doc went on to tell them about the $100,000 the townspeople and ranchers had been raising for five years to build a new courthouse. He mentioned that Bullet Richards got it all and they hired Doc to find him.

Snake-Eye was busy eyeing Angie and trying to figure out how to get her alone, away from Doc, and had tuned out Doc's story, until he heard the name "Bullet." He perked up and listened to the story Doc was telling then. His one eye gleamed with anticipation as he started mentally calculating this new development.

"What brings you to Dry Gulch?" Angie asked, coquettishly ducking her head and batting her eyes. A look, thought Duke, which was beyond ridiculous when tried by someone as obviously way past the age of someone who might be able to get away with it. Snake-Eye apparently did not feel the same, as he was gently stroking Angie's fingers as they lay on his thigh. Doc grunted, and echoed Angie's question, trying to draw Snake-Eye's attention away from Angie.

"Just wanderin' around the West," Snake-Eye lied, not wanting to reveal he was after the same man as Doc, but for a very different reason. He gloated to himself as he thought about catching Bullet with not only his share of the illicit poker game, but now with the takings from the Wyoming bank as well.

The next day, both gun fighters were up at the crack of dawn, and, after a hurried breakfast of biscuits and strong, bitter, black coffee at the hotel café, they headed out, looking for signs that Bullet had come in during the night. Snake-Eye pretended to be bored as he wandered down the street toward the general store, but he was watching Doc as he hurried to the livery stable to inquire if there were any new horses in town. Neither one of them was thinking about Angie, who was frantically going through her wardrobe, looking for something other than the frowsy barfly clothes she usually wore. She was hoping she could get one of her old gunfighter flames to ask her to go with him, and this time she would not turn him down! But, she needed to show that she was more than just a barfly – and was sure she had some respectable clothes somewhere.

As Doc strode up to the doorway of the livery, Bullet was sneaking out the back door near the corral. He saw Doc enter, and in his haste to hide behind the water trough, he tripped over an old saddle someone had dropped outside the back of the livery. The crashing sound caught Doc's attention and he hurried toward the noise, six gun drawn at his side. Snake-Eye noticed Doc's hurried movement and ran toward the stable, thinking that Doc might have found Bullet.

The three men, each aware of only one other, spent the next few minutes peering around bales of hay, the water trough, and other livery stable equipment, hoping to see something that would give away the position of the others. Doc was looking for an unknown man, but one he thought was Bullet, Snake-Eye was looking for Doc, and Bullet was trying to hide from Doc. He did not see Snake-Eye come up behind him until it was too late. "Put em up!" Snake-Eye whispered, "Or I will shoot you right now!" "And be quiet, I don't want Doc to find us just yet!"

Bullet jerked around and found himself staring down the barrel of Snake-Eye's six-shooter. "Quick, get over here, Doc can't see us back behind this wagon. He thinks you are still out by the corral." Bullet did as Snake-Eye said, seeing as how he really did not have a choice. "Look, Snake, I can get you your money now," Bullet started to say. "Shhh. Not here!" Snake-Eye looked back over the boot of the wagon to see where Doc was. He saw Doc's back as he crept closer to the water trough. Snake-Eye and Bullet then sneaked out the front of the livery stable, down between it and the building next door, then into the track in back leading behind the hotel, general store, and jailhouse. Once they got behind the hotel, Snake-Eye grabbed Bullet, shoved his gun in his face and growled, "I want my money and half of what you got in the Wyoming robbery or I tell Doc where you are!"

"You're not telling Doc anything, Snake-Eye. Now you jest put that gun down and back off Mr. Bullet there." Both of them turned and stared in shock at Angie, who held a shotgun leveled at Snake-Eye's head. "Now, Angie, put that down before you hurt yourself!" Snake-Eye took a step toward Angie, who waved gun and tightened her finger on the trigger. "I may not be a crack shot like you, but this here is a shotgun and you ain't that far away, I figure I can do some serious damage with it, so once again, back away!" Angie looked like she might really pull the trigger. Snake-Eye lowered his gun and stepped back.

"Now what ya gonna do, Angie? I thought we had somethin' there last night." Snake-Eye whined a bit, looking from the shotgun to Angie's face.

"I thought we did, too, but then I figured Mr. Bullet here has somethin' more – at least $100,000 more – and I think he would be a better choice for me to run off with. Right, Mr. Bullet?" She swung the barrel back and forth between them.

"Well, actually, Angie, I figure neither one of these boys has anythin' you will be wantin' seein' as how both of them are headed for the jailhouse!" They all three turned and stared as Doc stepped out from the shadows, his gun aimed at Snake-Eye and Bullet.

"And, Angie, I would put that gun down right fast unless you are plannin' on joinin' them in there." Duke, wearing a tin sheriff's star, stepped out beside Doc.

Snake-Eye and Bullet went to jail, the money was recovered and the townspeople of Deadwood were able to build their new courthouse and Doc went back to patrolling Montana and Wyoming Territories, looking for bank robbers. What about Angie and Duke? Why, they got married, of course. It seems Angie was just looking for a big, strong man to take care of her, and Duke, who had always been jealous of her past life as the riverboat princess with men chasing after her all the time, finally realized that those days were long gone!

Kids' Halloween Stories

The first story in this series, "Trial Run," was inspired by the Halloween decorations we put up in the front yard every year. We had an eight-foot tall blow-up witch that the neighborhood kids named Luanda. She was not a scary witch and I decided I needed to write her story.

The other two stories were written in response to a prompt-driven children's story contest. The prompt was *spider*.

Trial Run

Luanda was always late, even when whatever event she was attending was in her own home. She was always stopping on the way, distracted by something like a feather under the couch, then getting the dust mop out and dusting the room, then on to something else and before you knew it, she was lost again. This time her sister, Eloise, in the kitchen slowly stirring the contents of the old black and warped cast iron pot, was more than usually irritated at Luanda's tardiness. She needed to add the fourth ingredient at just the right time or the recipe would fail. Luanda said she knew where she could find that special ingredient and had gone to look for it.

It was almost the first of October and the leaves outside were turning and falling from the trees. It was much cooler in the evenings now, and Luanda loved to sit on the porch, swinging in the old creaky swing, just watching the day go by. That was where she was right now, having forgotten all about Eloise in the kitchen with her pot. Something dashed out of the trees just at the edge of their property, catching Luanda's eye but disappearing before she actually saw it. For some reason, the motion in the trees reminded Luanda that she was supposed to be looking for something for Eloise. She jumped up from the swing, setting it to thrash wildly on the rusty chains holding it to the porch roof, and scurried into the house.

"For gosh sakes, Luanda," Eloise scolded as her sister came into the kitchen through the pass-through pantry from the dining room. "You know I need that ingredient at exactly the right time, or this recipe will fail!" She turned, taking the long wooden spoon out of the pot, dripping over the top of the wood burning stove, the drips sizzling and popping from the heat. "Now look what you made me do! I just cleaned the stove, too!" She was looking at the mess she was making and she did not see that Luanda had her hand out, a small jar in it, a smile on her face.

"Here it is, and just in time, too." Luanda shook the tiny jar, rattling the contents to get Eloise's attention.

"Humph! I don't know how you do it, but you always do come through in the end." Eloise smiled indulgently and took the jar from Luanda, opened it and carefully sprinkled the contents into the pot. There was a faint hissing sound as she slid the spoon back into the pot and started stirring again. "Thanks, honey. I am sorry I yelled at you. It is just that this is so important right now and you do tend to get distracted very easily, especially this time of the year."

"I think I saw Skink out there just this side of the trees." Luanda changed the subject, "It looked like he was running from something, or maybe just running because it is a beautiful evening for running," she grinned, the thought of dashing about in the trees on a cool evening delighting her. "I'm going to go see if I can find him."

Eloise shook her head, smiling quietly into the pot. She loved her younger sister so much, even if she was a scatterbrain. Satisfied with the cooking progress to this point, she took the spoon out, this time carefully putting it in the spoon rest so she did not drip on the stovetop again. The big cookbook with the pages yellowed and curling in places was on the counter next to the stove and she consulted it, running her long, green, pointed fingernail down the list of ingredients to make sure she had all of them in order.

As Luanda came back into the kitchen, cradling a large black cat in her arms, Eloise gave the pot one final stir, turned, and said, "I am so glad we decided to use crushed newt eggshells instead of eye of newt, aren't you, sister? They work just as well and we didn't have to boil the newts first." Eloise smiled at Skink and rubbed his head, which was tucked into Luanda's elbow. "Well, let's get going, we have to get in at least four trial runs before the big night!"

The girls hurried out of the kitchen, swirling their long, black skirts behind them. Once they had their pointed black hats settled on their heads, they turned to the two long broomsticks leaning against the door jam. Eloise picked them up, went back to the kitchen, and, first dipping the brushy ends in the pot of flying potion and swirling them around, handed one to her sister. They settled themselves on the dusty brown broom shafts, Skink behind Luanda, and waddled out the back door onto the porch. As the sun sank below the tree level, they shot off the porch, flying low at first, then, a bit wobbly, up toward the darkening sky, shouting and laughing. "I love the first trial run every season!"

"Me, too!"

Lucky Spider

Magic is in the air every year around the end of October. This is the time when black cats talk, broomsticks fly, and lucky spiders are, well, lucky. It is Halloween night and this year would be the first year that Spiky Spider was allowed to go Trick-or-Treating with his friends. He just knew this would be his lucky year. As he was getting ready to meet his friends, Spiky was thinking about all the candy he would be bringing home and did not notice the broomstick twitching in the corner of the kitchen. He scurried along the edge of the room, dragging his trick-or-treat bag along behind him. Just as he disappeared under the door, the broomstick jumped up and flew after him, smacking the door and falling down.

"Oh, come on, Princess, you can do better than that!" Max, a slinky black cat who was watching from across the room, said, chuckling in his whiskers.

"My name is Princeton, not Princess!" the broomstick retorted. "And that silly spider caught me off guard. I wasn't expecting him this early." Princeton huffed and swept back across the floor to his corner.

"You know you only have one day left to get rid of the spiders in this house and on Halloween spiders are lucky." Max went on to tease Princeton, the magic broomstick. Princeton was a young broomstick, and in order for him to gain all his magic powers, he had to sweep all the spiders in the house outside before midnight on Halloween. This year was his last chance to gain his powers. If he failed, he would never become a flying magic broomstick.

Princeton slumped down on his straw and concentrated on how he was going to get Spiky and his friends out of the house before midnight. He just had to gain his powers so he could be a flying broomstick next year and give the witches rides through the night. He thought and he thought. Suddenly, he had an idea! Ignoring Max, who was dosing on the windowsill, he swept out of the kitchen, trailing straw pieces behind him.

In the meantime, Spiky had met up with his friends in the mudroom behind the kitchen. "Hi guys! This is going to be so much fun! I have to be careful, though, because I think Princeton is after me – and probably all of you, too!"

"Yes, but you know spiders are lucky on Halloween," said Herbie, the spider that lived behind the washer, his eight eyes nervously looking around the room.

"I think that is an old spider's tale," Selena, the spider from under the windowsill, said. "My mom used to tell me that every year until the year Princeton's big brother swept her right outside on Halloween morning!"

"Well, no matter what, we need to be careful!" Spiky grinned at Selena and blushed as much as a spider could blush. (He had kind of a spidy crush on her.)

The spider children gathered up their trick-or-treat bags and cautiously crept out of the mudroom into the kitchen, keeping all their eyes peeled for Princeton. Max opened one eye, peered lazily at the spiders as they crossed the floor, then closed his eye and pretended to be asleep again.

"Nobody in here but lazy old Max." Selena whispered.

Just as they reached the corner where Princeton usually sat, Max jumped down from the window, arched his back, and hissed at the spiders, scaring them silly. "Hey sssssspidersssss," he hissed, "Better watch out! Princess is on the prowl, looking for you!"

"Stop calling him Princess, Max! His name is Princeton." Spiky did not like it when Max teased the broomstick, even if Princeton wanted to sweep Spiky outside. During non-magic times of the year, Spiky and Princeton had become great friends. The straw bundle on the bottom of the broomstick was a fun place for a spider to play hide and seek with his friends.

"Hey! Look over there! That big black pot must have some good Halloween treats inside!" Herbie started crawling over to the counter so he could climb up and see what was in the pot. Selena and Spiky followed, dragging their sacks behind them. Up, up, they went, straight up the front of the cupboard to the countertop. Just as they were crawling up the side of the black pot, the door to the living room slowly opened and Princeton stuck his head in, looking around for the spiders.

"Spiky!" Princeton called out in a loud whisper, "I have an idea. Come here and I will tell you how we can both get what we want this Halloween!"

"Don't believe him, Spiky!" Herbie was scared that Princeton was trying to trick them. Selena didn't say anything, but watched Spiky to see what he would do. Max just grinned, thinking he knew what Princeton was up to.

Spiky trusted his friend, though, and crawled over to see what he had to say. They whispered together for a minute, then Spiky called Herbie and Selena over. Max was surprised to see the three spiders crawl up into the straw bundle just as Princeton started sweeping slowly to the back door.

"And stay out!" Princeton shouted as he shook his straw outside. "There! Mission accomplished! And now I get my full magic flying powers!" He jumped up and zipped around the room to show Max his new skills. Max shook his head and slowly walked through the door to the living room.

"OK, guys, you can come out now." Princeton said as Spiky, Herbie, and Selena crawled out of the straw bundle, dragging their full trick-or-treat bags with them. The bags were full of candy that Princeton had hidden for them. They scampered back into the mud room to eat their candy while Princeton swooped around and around the kitchen!

A Very Spider Halloween

"Ponce 'ponce time, grandma!" My three-year-old grandson was getting ready for bed the night before Halloween and was asking for a bedtime story. He hadn't quite mastered the words yet, but I knew 'Once Upon a Time' when I heard it from him.

"Ok, Jeremy, what kind of story do you want tonight? A princess story?" I grinned, knowing full well that Jeremy was not at all interested in princesses.

"No! Yuck! I want a spider story!" Halloween was on his mind after spending the evening helping his daddy hang some ghosts and skeletons in the hallway.

"Well, ok, but don't blame me if you get scared!"

"I won't get scared! I'm a big boy!"

"Once upon a time," I began the story as Jeremy settled back into the pillow.

There was a family of spiders living under a log in the forest. They were very nice spiders, but the children in the big house at the edge of the woods were scared of them. Whenever the spiders came out to play, the children ran away screaming, hurting the spiders' feelings. Then one October morning the spiders had an idea about how to make the children love them. They decided to have a Halloween party and invite the children!

"What fun this will be!" cried little Suzy Spider, the youngest member of the spider family. "We can play games, eat cake and candy, and show the children that we are really lots of fun to play with."

As Halloween got closer, the spiders were busy decorating their log home with lots of pretty webs. They stuck leaves and other small bits they found on the forest floor into the webs to make them festive for the party. They were trying to figure out how to invite the children to the party when they heard someone walking through the trees. Tommy Spider, Suzy's big brother, scampered up a branch so he could see who was in the forest. It was Skinch, the black cat that lived with the children! He could help the spiders! The children loved him.

"Hey!" Tommy called out when Skinch walked by the branch Tommy was sitting on. "Skinch, it's me, Tommy Spider!"

"Oh, hi, Tommy. I haven't seen you and your family lately. Where have you been?" Skinch sat down and curled his tail around by his feet. He and the spider family were old friends.

"We're getting ready for a Halloween party! We've been decorating our log home." Tommy looked around proudly at all the webs he and his family had made. "Do you think the children will come? We want to play with them, but they always run away when they see us." Tommy was really sad now, thinking of the children running away.

"I don't know, Tommy. The children think you and your family will bite them!" Skinch shook his head, sure that the children would not want to come to a spider party, even if it was Halloween.

"Please, Skinch, will you bring them? If they come with you, they might not be so scared of us. We won't bite them, we promise!" Suzy had crawled up on the branch beside her brother. All eight of her eyes were brimming with tears, and Skinch just hated to see anyone cry, especially little girls.

"Oh, OK, I will see what I can do." Skinch disappeared into the dark forest, leaving the spider brother and sister sitting on the branch. They scampered back down to the forest floor and rushed home to tell the rest of the family all about Skinch and his promise to bring the children to the party.

The next day was Halloween and the children were very excited as they got ready to go trick-or-treating. Their mother was cooking something in a big, black pot on the stove. She was stirring it with a long spoon, mumbling something that sounded like "Boil, boil, toil and trouble." The children thought that was kind of strange, but it WAS Halloween, after all, and lots of strange things could happen!

In fact, their cat, Skinch, had been acting really strange all day. He kept meowing at them, and running toward the forest, looking back at them as if he expected something. Their mother looked up from her pot, her eyes gleaming, and said, "Maybe he wants you to follow him into the forest." She picked up a broomstick and swished it across the floor, mumbling about spiders, cats, and Halloween.

"Let's go see what he wants!" The children ran off toward the woods behind Skinch. As they started into the trees, they stopped and looked around in wonder. There were silky, shimmery spider webs everywhere! "Wow, how pretty!" little Jane said, "Look, Billy! There are leaves and sticks in the webs – it looks like decorations for a party!"

"And look over there!" Billy pointed at a log covered in webs, "There is a whole family of spiders! They must have made all these webs!"

"Hey! I wonder if they did this for us?" Jane said, her eyes wide as she spotted a tiny cake and a whole bunch of candy near the log. "Do you think it is a spider Halloween party?"

"Yes, yes! A Spider Halloween Party!" Suzy, Tommy, and the rest of the spider family were jumping up and down in excitement. The children sat down on the forest floor and played with the spiders in the beautiful webs. Skinch curled up next to the log and went to sleep, a satisfied smile on his face.

All about Families

These stories all showcase different kinds of families or family events.

Defining Family

I came of age in a time of no heroes. Oh, there were comic book heroes, super-heroes, but no real heroes. Nobody to show me how life was to be lived. I lived in a box under a bridge. It was the only home I could remember. I had no family, no mom, no dad. It was just me and my box. My only role models were others like me: kids with no heroes. We spent our days trying to stay alive and our nights hiding from the bigger kids.

The summer nights were the best and the worst at the same time. The soft, balmy air made keeping warm much easier, but it also drew out all the crazies. The bigger kids seemed to swell even bigger in the summer night, and there were more of them. We did our best to stay in the shadows, hiding under the piles of old clothes and cardboard that came from nowhere and everywhere on those soft nights. In the winter, the piles protected us, but in the summer, they smothered us.

They weren't clean, either. Bugs that somehow came to life in the summer crawled all over us while we tried to be invisible, making us squirm, scratch, and sometimes sneeze. There were no bugs in the winter.

I was trying to get back to my box-room under the bridge unobserved one summer night when I first saw her, or rather, heard her. The stick she was dragging behind her scratched along the dirt, knocking a few old cans out of the way, causing a clatter I was sure could be heard by the big kids at the end of the alley.

"Shhh!" I motioned her to be quiet. I was not in the mood for a run-in with the big kids, who were hooting and hollering at something (or someone?) hunched over on the ground in front of them. They were facing away from the girl and me, and had not heard the clattering cans over their own noises.

As she got closer, I could see the girl was about my age, but not near as dirty or skinny as I was. She must be new. The new ones were always cleaner and fatter. Not that she was fat, not at all, but fatter than I was for sure. Her shoes fit, which meant they were probably her own shoes, not some cast-offs from the homeless shelter. They were dirty and one lace was missing, but they fit and I could see socks puddled around her ankles – they looked like they matched.

I ducked behind a trash bin, motioning her to follow me. The noise from the big kids at the end of the alley changed, dropped down a level. A couple of them turned and looked toward us, had they seen one or both of us? I heard footsteps, then someone shouted, "It's prolly just a cat – come on back! We have a real live one here!"

Uh-oh. That meant they had surrounded one of the little kids and were tormenting him or her. "Shhh," I said again as the new girl slid behind the bin with me. "You don't want them to find us back here."

"But, shouldn't we go help whoever they have?" She crouched down, putting her lips close to my ear, tickling it with the words she breathed.

"Not unless you want to be tortured." Sitting back on my heels, I looked at her in the near darkness. Some weak light crept around the black shape of the partially open back door of a restaurant, muted noise tumbling out with it. Up close, she was dirtier than I first thought, with streaks of something dark running down her cheeks, like dirty tears. Her lips were cracked and swollen, with tiny spots of red in places. Blood, or lipstick? I couldn't tell. She tucked her head in and clutched the front of her shirt closed in her small hands, partially hiding a dirty white strap crossing her exposed shoulder.

"Oh, um, are you OK?" I reached out and brushed my fingers along the yellow edges of an old bruise fading along her jaw line. Instead of jerking her head back, she sighed and leaned into the cup of my hand for a minute, then straightened up, her eyes widening for a moment, searching my face.

"How long have you been out here?" She pulled her head away and leaned out so she could see down the alley to where the big kids were starting to move away.

I poked my head out beside hers, noticed the kids moving away, and started to scoot out into the alley. "I don't know, forever, I guess. I don't remember anything else but being here. What about you? Where did you come from?"

We were both standing now, the sound of loose dirt hitting the alley floor as we brushed off our pants, muffling our still whispered words.

"Look! Is that the kid they were beating up?" She pointed and started walking toward a heap of what looked like dirty clothes at the end of the alley. The big kids were nowhere in sight.

I hung back a bit, trying to see into the shadows. "Careful! What if they come back?"

By now she was kneeling down at the bundle of rags, using her stick to poke at them. "Hey, are you OK?" Her soft voice melted into the darkness. She leaned closer as a tiny moan, muffled by the rags, escaped. "It's OK; we won't let them hurt you anymore."

I knew it was a bad idea, but I could not stop her. She tended that little kid all night in my box under the bridge. It was barely big enough for me, but that did not stop Diana. She told me her name as we dragged the kid away from the alley and into my box. He was more hungry and scared than he was hurt, but Diana figured he needed some rest in a safe place. Not that my box was very safe, but it was better than the open alley.

I spent the night pacing and looking out for the big kids. They mostly left the kids under the bridge alone, though. There were about 20 of us, all smaller kids, all living in boxes or under cardboard sheets. Once we made it here, to our flimsy homes, the big kids pretty much stayed away. They preferred a kid all alone to a bunch of kids all at once.

"I'm called Boy-Boy." The kid told us when Diana asked what his name was. He said he was out looking for food yesterday with some other little kids from a couple blocks over when the big kids found him. He had stopped to check out a dumpster and the other kids kept going. By the time he noticed they were gone, it was too late.

"Diana?" I stuck my head into the box, only to see Boy-Boy and Diana sound asleep, curled next to each other. It reminded me of something; a quick memory that was gone as fast as it appeared, leaving me sad for some reason. I sat down outside the box again, tired from no sleep, but also hungry.

An hour later, as I prowled through the alleys behind the bars and restaurants near my bridge, I wondered about Diana and Boy-Boy. Would they still be there when I got back? Part of me hoped they would not be; I did not want to be responsible for anyone else. On the other hand, it was nice to have someone else to talk to, someone who was not trying to hurt me or take my food. Just then, a door creaked open and I ducked behind a dumpster, my legs shaking as I realized just how close I had come to being seen. I heard a sound, like rustling plastic, as if someone put a bag of trash on the ground, and then I smelled cigarette smoke.

I hunkered down, making myself as small as possible and waited for whoever it was to finish the cigarette and go back inside the restaurant. Once the door closed again, I eased the dumpster lid open, hoping for some fresh breakfast leftovers. There was nothing in the bin, but I did see the handles of a plastic trash bag peaking around the side of it. I smelled the warm cinnamon and icing before I opened the bag. Three whole, individually wrapped cinnamon rolls. These were fresh, not leftovers! Throwing a last cautious glance at the closed door, I grabbed the bag and ran off toward my bridge.

The three of us licked the sticky icing off our fingers, not wanting to lose a bit of the sugary treat. I leaned back against the cement pillar holding up the bridge, patted my stomach, and sighed. It was a big cinnamon roll and it filled me up. I was ready for a nap. Boy-Boy and Diana said they would go out in a little while and see if they could find more food for later in the day. They, too, were full from the cinnamon rolls and nobody felt like moving just then. I heard them quietly talking as I dozed off, the lack of sleep and the warm cinnamon roll catching up to me.

Footsteps woke me awhile later; I jumped up and slipped behind the pillar I had been resting against. Then I heard voices, words like "last night," "dumpster," and "sandwiches" coming through my sleep-fogged brain. I stepped out to watch Diana and Boy-Boy approaching, a plastic bag like the one I found the cinnamon rolls in earlier hanging from Boy-Boy's hand.

"Hey, did you find some more cinnamon rolls?" My stomach growled at the thought.

"No, but we did find three, whole, sub sandwiches! They were right next to the dumpster we hid behind last night."

"Wow. Do you think someone is putting them out just for us?" I reached into the bag and took out a package about eight inches long, wrapped in white paper. I could smell lunchmeat and mustard as I peeled the paper off the fresh bun. When I took the first bite, something dribbled down my chin. Whoever made the sandwich must have used some kind of oil for the dressing. My mind flashed on something, but the image was too fleeting for me to catch. I shrugged and took another bite.

"I don't know, but it does seem strange that there were three cinnamon rolls this morning and now three sandwiches this afternoon, doesn't it?" Diana nibbled at the lettuce, meat, and cheese that hung over the sides of the bun. Boy-Boy had already finished his sandwich and was licking the oil and mustard off his lips.

"I think we should go knock on that door and see who answers!" Diana gathered up the sandwich wrappers, stuffed them into the plastic bag, and started walking back toward the alley.

"No! It could be a trap! What if it is Social Services? And anyhow, it's going to be dark soon, the big kids will be out looking for trouble." I took the bag from her and tossed it on the ground behind my box with all the other trash I had thrown there.

We spent the evening staying close to the bridge, playing a game similar to kick-ball, but with no ball, just bags of trash. A group of big kids walked by across the street, calling out to us, but not coming close enough to catch us. There were several other little kids under the bridge, too. Safety in numbers.

Early the next morning, Diana left the shelter of the box and slipped down the alley toward the dumpster. She waited until she heard the door open, and then stepped out from the shadows. A man was just putting a trash bag down next to the bin; Diana could smell the cinnamon.

"Why are you doing this?"

The man started at her voice, "Oh! I didn't see you there. I just wanted you and your friends to have some good, hot food, that's all." He looked nervous, checking the door behind him as he spoke. He picked up the bag and held it out toward Diana. "Here, take it before some other kids come along and find it."

Boy-Boy poked me awake, asking where Diana was. I was sleeping outside my box, under a sheet of cardboard. There was not enough room inside for all three of us. "I don't know, isn't she inside?" I gestured toward the box.

"Duh, no. Would I be asking you if she was?" Boy-Boy huffed his annoyance. "I'm hungry. Are you going to get some food or do you want me to go this time?"

I figured Boy-Boy was only about seven or eight years old, but kids get wise fast when living on the streets. I didn't know for sure how old I was, but I think I was around 11. Almost a big kid. I didn't want to think about being a big kid and picking on someone like Boy-Boy. "I'll go. You stick around here and see if you can find us another box – or at least a bigger one. With three of us now in our family, we will need more room."

His eyes got wide and shiny. "Are you saying we are family? You want to be my family?"

"Yeah, Boy-Boy. I do want to be your family. We need to stick together out here." I ruffled his hair, feeling a lot older than I should have. "Now go find us another home."

"Hey, guys!" Diana called out from across the street, "I have breakfast!" She waited for a car to pass, and then darted over to us. "Look, cinnamon rolls again! And, there are three cartons of milk, too!"

After breakfast, we scouted around and found another box, a bit smaller than my original one, but cleaner. It would do nicely for one person. We took it back to the first box and lashed the two of them together with twine we found wrapped around some boards behind the bridge pillars. We felt proud of our new, fancy, two-room home. Boy-Boy and I would sleep in the bigger box and Diana took the newer, smaller one.

We talked about the man who was leaving us food, and wondered what he wanted. None of us had any real trust for adults, and we figured that someday he would demand something from us. However, we were also tired of digging in dumpsters and then living in fear that someone would take our food from us, so decided that until the man demanded something in return, we would take his food.

That evening I went to see if he was going to leave us some more of those great subs. Sure enough, there was a bag sitting by the side of the dumpster.

"Hey kid! Whatcha got there?" I was almost to the end of the alley when I heard a big kid call out to me. There were six of them, all leaning against the fence surrounding the property on the right side of the alley, just across from me. I had been so involved in the delicious smells coming from the bag that I forgot to watch out for them.

I opened the bag, made a face, and then tossed it into a pile of trash, hoping the big kids would think it was nothing and let me go. "Nothing, just some garbage I picked up, I thought it had some food in it, but it doesn't." I stepped into the street, not looking at the big kids, pretending as if I did not have a care in the world.

"Yeah, you sure?" One of the kids separated himself from his friends and started toward me. Just then, Diana stepped away from the group of little kids watching us from across the street.

"Hey, Marty!" she called out. "Boy-Boy found another box! We can each have our own room! Hurry up, come and see it!"

The big kid stopped and looked over at her; he turned as though he was going to cross the street, then stopped again. "Hey girlie! I haven't seen you around here before. Why don't you come over here and hang out with us? We are a lot more fun than the little kid losers over there."

I ran as fast as I could across the street while the big kid was taunting Diana, who remained right where she was, just outside the little kids' camp. Boy-Boy stood behind her. The three of us moved back toward the center of the camp, where about 15 more little kids were standing around, nervously watching the big kids across the street.

"Ah, you're all a bunch of losers!" The big kid shouted as he turned back toward the pile of trash where I had thrown the bag of sandwiches. His friends moved out away from the fence, joining him. I cringed, knowing they were about to find our dinner.

"Time to move along, kids." A voice came from deeper in the alley. A man dressed in white chef's pants and a white t-shirt stepped out from behind the dumpster. He had a frying pan in his hand and he casually slapped his other hand with it as he walked toward the group of bullies. The big kids scattered, running down the street at the end of the alley, away from the bridge.

The man nodded at us, turned, and walked back toward the dumpster and the open doorway beyond it.

That night, as Diana, Boy-Boy, and I ate our sandwiches, we talked about the man, the big kids, and most of all, our new family. As it turned out, there were heroes all around us.

Emma Sue's Angels

When folks sat around and talked about that summer, they always said the same thing: "It was unseasonably hot that year." When I heard that, I knew they were going to start talking about Emma Sue, the sister that disappeared.

Emma Sue was five years old that summer. She was small for her age, and kind of sickly, but that did not stop Mamm from expecting her to pull her own weight in the fields, just like the rest of us. There were six of us, all girls. I was the oldest at 12. Emma Sue was not the youngest, that was Polly Mae, she was three. We all worked in the fields, picking celery. It was hard work, cutting those tough stalks right at the base. Mamm would not let the younger ones have the sharpest knives because she was afraid they would cut themselves, but it was harder to cut celery with the dull knives.

Emma Sue especially hated it and was always sneaking off to play in the rows between the stalks. She had a great imagination and she was always talking about playing with angels in between the celery rows. We figured that was just talk, Emma Sue making stuff up so she would not get in trouble when she ran off to play. Mamm loved angels and she did not fault Emma Sue for wanting to play with them.

"Emma Sue!" Mamm called quietly so the foreman would not hear her and know that Emma Sue was missing again. "Where have you gotten to? You are way behind in your cutting. You come out now, hear me?" Mamm looked around but could not see Emma Sue's faded blue bonnet poking up above the rows of celery. She could see everyone else bent over in the fields, busily hacking at the base of the plants, but not Emma Sue.

"Now where has that girl gotten herself to?" Mamm muttered as she tried to keep looking while she kept slicing at the celery plants. "She is going to get a whupping for certain when she comes back."

We all kept working; the foreman was mean and we did not want to feel his whip lashing our backs as we worked under the hot sun. It would not be long before we stopped for our bread and cheese lunch, so we just wiped the stinging sweat out of our eyes and kept on cutting celery, listening for the whistle so we could stop to eat.

Emma Sue was still missing when the whistle finally signaled our lunch break. Mamm looked all up and down the rows, calling her name over and over. The only one who had not been bent over in the celery rows all morning was the foreman on top his big horse. Mamm finally got up the courage to ask him if he saw Emma Sue slip away.

"Nah, that girl is slick. She proll'y ran away. Don't matter much, though, y'all still has to pick the same …Emma Sue or not." The foreman trotted off toward the shade and a cool drink, leaving Mamm standing alone in the field.

"Mamm!" Polly Mae said, "Pretty!" We all looked out at the celery field to where she was pointing. A huge pair of white wings beat slowly just above the tops of the celery. Suddenly, they started glowing white gold, so bright we had to look away. When we looked back, they were gone.

Nobody ever saw Emma Sue again.

Jenna and the Burglar

Jenna knew she was not supposed to take the short cut home from school, but she figured that this one time it be would OK since nobody saw her turn off at the corner. Her big brother and his friends all ran ahead of her right after they left the schoolyard, even though their mom said he was supposed to walk her home every night. Jenna didn't care, she did not like having Joel and his creepy friends around. They always teased her and made her cry. It was much better walking home alone, and if she took the short cut, Joel would not be able to find her in case he remembered he was supposed to walk her home.

She scuffed her worn tennis shoes along the sidewalk as she headed toward the trees that backed up the post office and general store. Her house was just on the other side of the trees, and she only had to cut through a small part of the much larger forest to get home. The sun was hot and she knew it would be cooler once she got under cover of the trees so she hurried along, not noticing the puffy clouds with smoky grey undersides building up quickly on the horizon behind her. By the time she reached the edge of the forest, the previously slight breeze was much stronger, blowing her long brown hair into her eyes.

"Hey! Where's Jenna?" one of Joel's friends shouted at Joel, who was busy looking into the general store window. He pretended he was looking at the display, but he was really looking past it, hoping to see the store owner's daughter, Maxie, who was working behind the counter inside. "Huh?" Joel started. "What do you mean? She's right behind us."

"No, she's not." His friend replied.

Joel looked back up the road toward the school building. He did not see Jenna anywhere. "Oh crap! Mom's gonna kill me." Joel hated being his little sister's keeper, but knew that his mom would be mad if he did not walk her home every day. "You guys go ahead on home, I'll go back and get Jenna." He turned and started walking back up the sidewalk toward the school, scuffing his feet on the sidewalk in the same manner his little sister had done a few minutes ago on another sidewalk.

Jenna stepped off the roadway into the trees as a gust of wind blew past, carrying an old envelope, some dirty leaves, and a sheet of newsprint with it. She brushed her hair out of her eyes and looked back at the rattle of the leaves and paper, shuddered a little when she saw the ominous clouds, and then turned back to the trees. "I better hurry," she thought, "it might rain and I don't want to get wet." She moved quickly onto the faint path between the trees, shifting her backpack around from her shoulder to her back so it was easier to walk faster. It was starting to get a little darker with the approaching storm and Jenna wondered for a minute if she had made the wrong decision by taking the forbidden short cut. Soon she was hurrying along, secure in the woods she knew so well. She felt smug about slipping away from Joel and was looking forward to seeing his face when he got home and she was already there.

Even with a storm brewing, the forest was relatively quiet. The wind had not penetrated the trees yet, and Jenna found herself enjoying her walk through the growing twilight. It was peaceful and she slowed her pace a bit to look around at the surrounding trees and bushes, hoping to see a rabbit or maybe even a fox. She almost forgot about the storm, Joel, and the fact that she was disobeying a direct order from her mom about walking through the woods alone. That's why, when she first heard a rustling in the bushes ahead of her, she didn't react immediately, but when the rustle was followed by a large boom of thunder, she jumped and screamed a little. She thought she heard something else, like a voice calling out, but could not be sure because of the crashing thunder and her own slight scream. She hurried on toward home, more watchful than before.

Joel looked all over the schoolyard, even went back into the school, calling Jenna's name every once in a while. "Where could she be? I was sure she was right here when we left." He thought as he headed back through the schoolyard gate and started down the street toward the post office. He saw old Mr. Guthrie coming out of the post office and asked him if he had seen Jenna.

"Why, no, I haven't," Mr. Guthrie replied, "But you better get on home now, there is a heck of a storm comin' on. You don't want to get wet!" He started toward his car, parked on the street a few feet away, but turned back to Joel. "Oh, yeah! You might want to tell your mom that I heard Sara Jean over to the café tellin' about a burglar she heard about from Old Lady Petrie. Said the burglar broke into her sister's house and stole a TV! Tell your mom to be sure and lock up the house when she ain't at home." With that, he got in the car, started it up, and drove slowly off, both hands firmly on the wheel, head held high, back straight.

Joel just stood there looking after the car, wondering just whose sister had her house broken into; Old Lady Petrie or Sara Jean. He shook his head and started toward home, worrying about Jenna and how she managed to get by him and his friends. He figured she got ahead of them somehow, and was already home. Boy, was he going to let her have it when he got home.

Because of the wind, now rustling through the treetops and making a lot more noise, Jenna did not hear the footsteps coming toward her on the path. Her view of the last section of the woods was blocked by a curve in the path so she was totally surprised when a man stepped out of the trees just ahead of her. He was big, and was looking back over his shoulder, which is why he was just as surprised to see Jenna as she was to see him. "Oh!" she gasped when she looked up and almost ran right into him.

"Oh!" he answered, "Where did you come from?"

"I, uh, I just came…" she pointed back behind her, "from there….."

"Humph!" the man said, peering closely at Jenna. "Where are you going?"

"There…" She pointed behind the man, clearly flustered. She did not know what to say, and seemed to have forgotten where she was headed.

"Well, then," the man said, "maybe you should get going … to 'there' before someone figures out you are gone. Are you supposed to be in these woods during a storm?"

"N-n-no," Jenna stammered, but the man was not listening. He was looking back the way he came again. "What are you looking for?" Jenna asked timidly.

"Oh, no—nothing. You had better get on home, young lady. It's going to rain soon." He started to move past Jenna on the path, but she stuck out her hand and stopped him.

"Don't you want to get out of the rain, too? You can come to my house if you want. I live just over there, past the trees." Jenna knew she should not be talking to strangers, let alone inviting them home, but she felt sorry for the man. He seemed so lost and maybe even a little scared. She wasn't afraid of him anymore, she just wanted to help him.

"Such a nice little girl!" The man smiled at her. "Thank you for the invitation, but I really don't think it would be such a good idea for me to go back there." He shifted a pillowcase on his shoulder that Jenna had missed before. It seemed to be filled with some bulky objects. Jenna gasped again, "It must be all his stuff! He must be homeless!" She thought, and was even more determined to help this poor man out of the storm.

"Come on, my mom will be home from work soon and she makes really good vegetable soup! I bet you are hungry, aren't you?" Jenna hoped that the offer of warm food would change his mind.

'No, I am not hungry, but thanks again. I must be going now, before the rain hits. You get on home, too!" He chuckled, then hefted the pillowcase on his shoulder again, and walked around Jenna. He was whistling when he walked up the path into the woods.

Jenna shrugged, and then headed off toward home. She felt bad for the man, but knew she tried her best to help him. In a few minutes she saw her back yard through the trees and broke into a run. The first raindrops hit her head and she wanted to get inside before she got really wet.

Joel walked in through the open front door of his house, calling out Jenna's name.

"Jenna! Did you leave the door open?" There was no answer. He looked in the kitchen, and then went on to the den – where he noticed that something was wrong. The desk lamp was tipped over on the floor, and several books were pulled from their places on the shelves.

"What happened here? Jenna! Are you here?"

"What's all the hollering for?" Joel's mom walked into the house, dropping her purse and keys on the hall table. "Hey, what happened in here?" She exclaimed as she walked into the den. "Where is Jenna?"

"I don't know! She snuck by me after school, I thought for sure she was ahead of me and already home. I just got here and found this mess in here. Jenna is not here!" Joel was looking around frantically, trying to figure out what was going on. Who made the mess? Where was his sister?

"Wait a minute, you don't suppose…" Joel was wondering as he gazed around the room.

"Suppose what?" His mother asked.

"Mr. Guthrie told me there was a burglary in town; he said he heard about it at the café."

"Oh, Joel, don't listen to that gossip . . . . where is the VCR? …and those movies that were next to it?" She was looking around the room as she spoke.

'Oh, man, we have been robbed!" Joel cried. "What else is missing?"

"Jenna!" they both said at the same time, staring at each other with wide, frightened eyes.

"What?" Jenna said as she came in through the back door.

Joel turned and stared at Jenna as if she was a ghost.

"Where did you come from?" he asked, still shaken and trying to figure out what was going on.

"I um, well; I took the short cut through the woods. I would have been here before you, but I stopped to talk to a nice homeless man. I invited him home for some of your delicious vegetable soup, mom, but he said no." Jenna rushed all this out in one big breath, hoping they would miss the part about taking the short cut. "He was really nice, but I knew he was homeless because he had a pillow case full of stuff, probably everything he owned!" She added, hoping they would share her concern for the nice man in the woods.

"More likely a bunch of stuff WE owned!" Joel sighed. "Oh Jenna, you made friends with a burglar! We were robbed today! Our VCR and some movies are gone. He probably wanted to use them with the TV he stole earlier from Old Lady Petrie's sister. Or Sara Jean's sister."

In Sickness and in Health

Somebody once said that rain on your wedding day was good luck. Lucy could not figure out why anyone would think that as she looked out through the rain-streaked window. All she could see was mud. The road was muddy, the yard was muddy, and the porch was even covered with muddy tracks. Lucy sighed, her chin resting in hand as she idly blew a long, perfectly straight strand of red hair out of her eyes. She wasn't exactly thrilled about the wedding to start with, and now the rain made things even worse. Lucy's brother, Todd, was marrying her best friend tomorrow, an event Lucy considered the biggest betrayal of all time. How could this happen?

Todd, Lucy's brother, older by only 11 months, was also Lucy's hero. She had looked up to him and was so proud of everything he did. Todd was tall and handsome, while Lucy was short and plain. Todd was popular, played football, was captain of the debate team and was considered the BMOC throughout their high school years. He graduated a year ahead of Lucy, who had only a few casual friends and one best friend, spent her high school years working on the school newspaper, her straight red hair usually pulled back in a sloppy pony tail and her glasses either on top of her head or hooked in the collar of her perpetual t-shirts. Now she felt like she was losing her only friend, even if her mom kept saying that now Cheryl would not only be her best friend, she would also be her sister. The only problem was, nobody but Lucy and Cheryl knew that Cheryl was dying.

The rain was turning to snow, which, if it stuck, would at least cover up all the mud. Lucy stood up from where she was curled up on the window seat. She needed to go talk to Cheryl one more time. This wedding was a mistake, she just knew it. She could not bear to see Todd hurt, and it killed her to know that Cheryl would probably be gone before the following summer.

"There you are." Lucy paused in front of the open door to the den, finding Cheryl sitting at the desk, her pale face illuminated by the computer screen on in front of her. "What are you doing?"

"Oh, hi, Luce. I am just doing some last minute research on our honeymoon trip. Did you know that Todd booked a 3-day Mexican Rivera Cruise?" Cheryl turned to face Lucy, her blue eyes sparkling and her cheeks slightly flushed, somehow making her look even paler under the pink tinge.

"Cheryl, you have to tell him. It is not fair to either of you." Lucy had said these same words to her so many times over the past few months, but Cheryl always blew her off with some flip remark. This time, however, Cheryl sighed, and answered Lucy, her tone resigned.

"Honey, I know you are worried about me and about Todd, but this is my decision, not yours. There is still a chance that a cure will be found in time. Besides, I know if I told him now, he will leave me and I am afraid of being alone if the cure is not found in time." A single tear slid down her right cheek, leaving a silver track back up to her eyes, not sparkling anymore, but swimming in unshed tears.

Lucy looked at her friend for a few minutes, watching the silent tears overflow and slip down to her chin. She finally turned and walked away.

The next morning the ground was covered with snow, the trees sheathed in ice from the rain the day before and dusted with snow, making the world dangerously beautiful. Lucy burrowed down into the bed, wishing the day was over and not just starting. She had made a decision during the night, a decision that she felt right about, but knew could change the lives of her brother and her friend. When the minister asked if anyone had any reason to oppose this marriage, Lucy planned to stand up.

The wedding was taking place in a small chapel, lit by candles and decorated simply with white orchids and satin ribbons. Cheryl's dress was also simple, a white silk sheath that accentuated her slim figure. Todd was one of those guys who looked great in a tuxedo, his white silk cummerbund fitted snuggly around his middle.

It was a small ceremony, with only a few friends and family members in attendance. There was a best man and Lucy fulfilled the role of bridesmaid. She nervously watched the minister as he droned on through the ceremony. All of a sudden, he spoke the words she was both dreading, and waiting for.

"If any of you can show just cause why they may not be married, speak now; or else forever hold your peace."

Lucy looked up and saw Cheryl looking right at her. Returning Cheryl's gaze, she stepped forward and raised her head to speak. "Wait," Cheryl said. "I have something to say."

Tumbleweeds

I noticed the tumbleweeds last Saturday morning. It was the first time I ever saw that many tumbleweeds all at once. They rattled toward me as I scuffed down the road past a field that looked as if it had been plowed a couple of weeks ago. I was heading home after spending the night with my best friend in the whole world. Every other time I spent the night at Juniper's house, her dad gave me a ride home after breakfast. This particular Saturday morning was not a usual day, however. In fact, her father probably would never give me a ride home again, and at the time I didn't think I would ever see Juniper again – my best friend in the whole wide world. However, I was wrong about that. Just like I was wrong about the tumbleweeds. I thought they were beautiful and free, the way I pictured my best friend, but they were really only scraggly, ugly, old weeds after all.

The day before my lonely walk home was the last Friday we would have free before school started, and Juniper and I were poking around in some boxes we found in the corner of the garage when we a found an old volume of Agatha Christie mystery stories. We knew they would be good stories, scary, but not too scary, because our sixth grade teacher last spring talked about Agatha Christie as one of the greatest mystery writers of all times. We thought she was exaggerating at the time, but still figured the stories in the old book would be fun to read. We were just getting settled in the armchair in the living room to start reading when I looked out the window and saw her mother coming toward the house from the barn. We originally wanted to go out to the loft, but we had been told to stay out of the barn by Juniper's dad.

"What are you girls up to?" Juniper's mom asked as she entered the living room.

"Nothing." We replied in unison, sliding secret looks to each other. "We found an old book and thought we would do some reading," Juniper mumbled.

"Reading? Really? On a fine afternoon like this? Why don't you go outside and play? It is, after all, your last day off before school starts." Mrs. Marsh seemed a bit anxious to get rid of us, but I figured it was just because we were in the living room and she wanted to watch her stories on TV.

"OK," Juniper surprised me by instantly agreeing with her mom. She jumped out of the chair, holding the book behind her back. "Come on, Sally, let's go outside." She winked at me.

"Stay out of the barn!" Mrs. Marsh admonished us as we sidled toward the front door, the book still held behind Juniper's back.

Of course, we went directly to the barn and ended up scaring ourselves reading those old mystery stories in the dimly lit loft. That's why, when we found *him* in the barn, we were too scared to look real close to see if we knew who he was. Actually, Juniper was the one who saw him when she came up the ladder after going to the outhouse. She had been gone for quite a long time and I was just going to look for her when I saw her poke her head up through the ladder hole in the loft floor. She looked sort of scared, like she had seen something that didn't belong there. I thought maybe she had seen the snake her brother said lived in the hole in the outhouse. (I never really believed him, though; why would a snake live in that stinky place?)

Juniper's long, brown hair was all twisted up with straw from the bales we had been lying on, and when she jerked her head toward the floor of the barn, little golden bits flew all over the place, making me sneeze.

"Shhhhhhh!" she put her finger over her mouth, "There's some guy down there!" Juniper's voice was scary – kind of shaky but excited all the same.

I peered over the edge of the loft and saw – nothing. "Where? I don't see anyone, Juniper, you're just trying to scare . . ."

"There, in the empty stall next to that dumb ole mule you like so much."

I leaned way out over the railing and thought I saw a deeper shadow in the murky light at the back of the barn. "Who is it? What's he doing there? Did he see you?" I whispered, even though I still wasn't sure I saw anything.

"I don't know who he is. I just thought I saw something when I went down the ladder. I went to over to the empty stall and looked in and saw him, all crumpled up. I was too scared to look closer."

"Oh, yeah? I bet it's one of your brother's friends trying to scare us. He's probably just pretending to be asleep or dead so we'll think he's just some ole tramp or something."

"I don't know. Maybe you're right." Juniper's voice was funny. Like she really wanted to believe me, but couldn't for some reason.

"But if I'm not . . .maybe we should tell your dad. He won't like some ole tramp sleeping in his barn."

"No! We can't tell anyone!" Juniper sounded frantic. "Remember, dad said for us to stay out of the loft because the ladder isn't safe? We'll get into trouble and you won't be able to come over here anymore."

We went back to the house without saying anything to anyone about the visitor in the empty stall.

Late in the night I heard someone yelling out in the yard and figured that Juniper's dad had found the tramp and kicked him out of the barn. I looked toward the window and was surprised at how light it was. Then I realized the light was a strange orange flickery kind of color. And the yelling was Juniper's dad all right The barn was on fire! I woke Juniper up and we hurried outside.

"Juniper, we better see if the tramp got out! He could burn up!" I was running toward her dad and the burning barn.

"Wait! He probably to out long ago. Don't say anything to Dad. You know how mad he'll get if he finds out we were in the barn earlier! He might even find a way to blame us for the fire!" Juniper just stood there watching as the flames licked up the side of the building.

"I called the fire department! They should be here right away." Juniper's brother, Billy, was running from the house behind us. He grabbed the garden hose and yelled for Juniper to turn it on. She looked around at the sound of his voice, but ignored his instructions. It was as if she was in a trance or something, moving in slow motion. I ran to the spigot at the edge of the garden and turned the water on. Juniper didn't say anything more, just watched awhile, then turned her back and walked back to the house.

"Cora, help me get some water to this side, where the hay rack is. I don't want the fire to spread any further!" Mr. Marsh was yelling and running to the side of the barn nearest the garden. Mrs. Marsh looked around like she hadn't heard him. She watched the fire for a few minutes, like Juniper had, then followed her daughter into the house.

"Sally, where's Juniper?" Mr. Marsh apparently noticed me for the first time.

"She went back in the house."

"You get in there with her! It's too dangerous out here! Billy, aim that hose over here!"

A pick-up truck skidded into the yard, and I recognized the hired hands from the neighboring farm as they jumped out and rushed to help Billy and Mr. Marsh with the fire. Some other people were running through the yard with buckets of water. With so much commotion going on, I was afraid of being trampled, so I went back into the house to find Juniper. She was so quiet in her bed, I figured she was asleep, even though I didn't know how she could sleep with so much racket going on. I watched the fire fighters from the bedroom window as they got things slowly under control. It was soon dark again without the flickery light from the fire and I went to bed, but I could not sleep. I also couldn't figure out why Juniper and her mom had acted so strangely.

In the morning, Juniper's mother got us up and told me I would have to walk home. Her husband wasn't there, and she said she didn't want to leave the farm. She hurried me out the door before breakfast and said that she and Juniper were going to be real busy for a while and not to come around for a few days. I tried to ask her why, but she shooed me out the kitchen door and sent me on my way.

I was curious (mom always said I was just plain nosey), so instead of starting home, I snuck around the side of the house to listen in at Juniper's bedroom window. Mrs. Marsh was talking to Juniper real fast like, but I couldn't hear Juniper saying anything.

"Your dad's been arrested. Seems your Uncle Bob showed up sometime yesterday or last night, passed out in the barn and burned up in the fire! The sheriff thinks your dad killed him in a fight and set the barn on fire in the process."

Juniper's Uncle Bob! So that was the 'tramp' we saw, and he was passed out, not sleeping! Why would Mr. Marsh kill his own brother? I tried to hear more, but I all I heard was Juniper mumbling something, then I heard her mom say, "We're leaving here today. We'll go to my sister's place. She'll know what to do." I didn't want to hear any more. My best friend in the whole world was leaving, and I'd probably never see her again. I ran out the gate and down the lane where the tumbleweeds slowly bumped down the blown-away little hill-tops between the plowed rows of the field.

When I got home, I looked for my mom to tell her what was going on, but she had already gone into town for the Saturday shopping. I went up to my room to get my diary. I remembered writing something in it a long time ago about Juniper's Uncle Bob, and I wanted to read it again. It was when I first met Juniper and her family. They had just moved to the farm next to ours and we were both 9 years old.

Three years before . . .

"I just met the nicest family. They moved into the old Jensen place down the road. There is a girl about my age named Juniper (what a funny name!), her big brother, her parents and another man. I think he is Juniper's uncle. I hope we are going to be friends. There isn't anyone else my age around here, except that weird kid up the road at the Monroe place – and he's a boy, so he doesn't count! . . ."

A few pages further on, I found the entry I was looking for. The ink was smeared on the page, but I could still read most of what I had written: *"Today Juniper and I were down by the creek when her uncle came by. He scared me because he was so quiet. I thought he was sneaking up on us, but Juniper said he was just a quiet kind of guy. I don't trust him, though. Dad said he was a fighter and a drinker, but mom told him to keep quiet about people he didn't know very well..."*

The door downstairs slammed and I knew mom was home. I threw the diary down on the patchwork quilt covering my bed and ran to see what she brought home from town. I also wanted to share my exciting news about Uncle Bob and the fire at Juniper's.

"Oh, Sally!" She sounded kind of out of breath. "I'm so glad you're home. I just heard in town about the fire and Mr. Marsh, and, oh, how horrible it must have been for you! Are you okay?"

"I'm fine, Mom! But we saw Uncle Bob in the barn before the fire. At least I think I saw him and Juniper said she saw him, but she didn't know it was her Uncle Bob! She thought he got out before the fire started." I was talking so fast I started to stumble over my words. Mom turned away and started to put the groceries away.

"Now, Sally, why don't you help me put these things away and just forget about what you and Juniper thought you saw. It really doesn't do any good to dwell on things we don't know anything about. Anyway the sheriff has arrested Mr. Marsh and everything will be over soon." She started to unpack the paper bags from the market, acting as if it was just like any other Saturday morning.

I wondered about Juniper and her family all afternoon, but mom changed the subject every time I brought it up. Finally, at dinner, I asked my dad what he heard about what had happened over at the Marshes the night before. Mom frowned and looked like she was about to say something when dad said, "Well, now, Sally, I was wondering when you were going to bring that up." His eyes twinkled the way they did when he was about to tell me something he knew mom wouldn't like. "I heard in town that Bob Marsh was back and I knew there would be trouble out at the Marsh place if Juniper's dad found out he was here."

"But why?" I wanted to know, "He was Mr. Marsh's brother. Why should there be a problem with him coming to visit his brother?"

"Honey, I told you we shouldn't be talking about things we know nothing about," mom said, firing a warning look at my father before looking at me. That was the end of Dad's discussion about the Marsh family troubles.

I had just barely dozed off later that night when I was startled awake by a rattle of gravel on my window. It took a few minutes for me to see who had thrown the gravel when I looked outside. It was very dark and the shadows beneath my window blended together. One shadow moved out into the weak light from my room. "Juniper! What are you doing here? I thought you and your mom left this morning?"

"I ran away, I couldn't stay with her anymore. Not after I found out what she did!"

"What? No, wait! I'm coming out! Don't go anywhere!" I opened my door and checked the hall. There was no light coming from under mom and dad's door, so I quietly moved downstairs to the kitchen and back door. When I got outside, Juniper was waiting for me next to the gate to the vegetable garden.

"Now tell me what is going on? What are you going to do?" I couldn't imagine running away and being without parents at our age. Juniper told me about her mom and Uncle Bob liking each other before her mom married her dad.

She said, "My dad was jealous of Uncle Bob, but he didn't kill his own brother!" Juniper said her mom did it and was letting her husband take the blame for her.

"But why?" I didn't understand why adults did such strange things.

"Because my mom was evil! She did it to get rid of both of them! I hated her!" Juniper was getting very upset and starting to shout.

"Shhhhh, you will wake up my parents. What are you going to do now?" I just realized she was referring to her mother in the past tense.

"Why, I'll live with you, of course," she replied, sweetly. Maybe too sweetly. "I know you would be like a sister to me and never hurt me the way they did."

A tumbleweed blew across the yard just then, and I jumped. It was an ugly thing, all scraggly and dirty.

Visiting Granny

Her veined and age splotched hands were barely distinguishable from the faded coverlet as she nervously picked at loose threads. Wisps of yellow-grey hair flew about her wrinkled face, her eyes darting from the window to the door as if she expected someone, or some*thing* to enter either opening. She gasped and jerked as a tiny sound, like pebbles on the screen, came from the window. The stained light green cotton bed jacket slid off her bony shoulders with the movement. Whatever made the sound was gone now, but she still stared fearfully at the window. It was growing dark outside and she became visibly more anxious as the light faded. She sighed, lips flapping over empty gums while her teeth rested in a glass of murky water on the bedside table. Her surprisingly bright blue eyes closed and she thought, "I'm afraid to sleep, afraid not to sleep."

In the hall outside the room, Alice wondered if granny would even know her if she went in. Ever since she came to this place, granny was getting really creepy and now that Alice had her driver's license her mom sent her every week instead of coming herself. It wasn't fair. She sighed heavily, pushing slowly on the door, hoping granny would be asleep.

Dusk was quickly giving way to darkness as the night crept closer to granny's window. She stirred restlessly in almost -sleep as she tried to remember what she was afraid of. The door moved slightly inward, fingers with green polish on the tips wrapped around the edge. Granny dragged herself awake and shrank back into the bed, staring at the door as shadowed eyes under blue and orange hair spikes peered from above the fingers. She thought she saw a flash of something, anger? defiance? in those eyes, then they were just Alice's eyes, sad and a bit resentful as she pushed the door wide and strode into the room. "Hi, Granny."

"Alice, what are you doing here? Where is your mother? I thought you mother was coming."

"Uh, Mom said she was busy and asked me to come." Alice's eyes skittered around the room, finally lighting on the dark window. She walked over to it and started to pull the yellowed curtain aside.

"No! Don't open it!" Granny was pushing herself down into the mattress, trying to get as far from the window as possible.

"What?" Alice turned to her grandmother, quickly dropping the curtain back into place, but not quick enough. Granny thought she saw something in the window before the curtain dropped. Something that looked shiny-red or slimy-red or maybe just red. Anyhow, whatever she thought she saw was enough to startle a soundless scream from her throat.

Disgusted, Alice flipped the curtain open again, watching granny, her back to the window. "See? Nothing there, you crazy old ..." The end of her sentence was swallowed up when the window exploded in a shower of silvery glass.

NOTE: The above story was written for a contest on character development. It won a $50 second place prize. I then used it as a basis for the first story in the next section: Visiting Granny (Revised). My writing partner, Rhonda Jackson took the story and turned it into our entry in the 2014 NYC Short Story contest, where we won Seventh Place.

Bonus Section: Collaborative Fiction

The following seven stories were written by Janie Sullivan and Rhonda Jackson as collaborative efforts. The first story is a revision of the last story in the previous section.

The second one is a story that we liked so much we decided to turn it into a crime novel. At this writing we have nine of 21 chapters completed. We hope to finish the novel by the end of the summer. Working title of the novel (same as the short story): *Alexis' Aggravation.*

Visiting Granny (Revised)

Her veined and age splotched hands were barely distinguishable from the faded coverlet as she nervously picked at loose threads. Wisps of yellow-grey hair flew about her wrinkled face, her eyes darting from the window to the door as if she expected someone, or some*thing* to enter either opening. She gasped and jerked as a tiny sound, like pebbles on the screen, came from the window. The stained light green cotton bed jacket slid off her bony shoulders with the movement. Whatever made the sound was gone now, but she still stared fearfully at the window. It was growing dusky outside, impending storm clouds not helping the gloomy late afternoon light, and she became visibly more anxious as the day faded. She sighed, lips flapping over empty gums while her teeth rested in a glass of murky water on the bedside table. Her surprisingly bright blue eyes closed and she thought, "I'm afraid to sleep, afraid not to sleep." She shivered.

In the hall outside the room, Alice wondered if Granny would even know her if she went in. Ever since she came to this place, Granny was getting really creepy and now that Alice had her driver's license her mom sent her every week instead of coming herself. It wasn't fair. She sighed heavily, pushing slowly on the door, hoping Granny would be asleep.

Afternoon was quickly giving way to dusk as the night crept closer to granny's window. She stirred restlessly in almost -sleep as she tried to remember what she was afraid of. The door moved slightly inward, fingers with green polish on the tips wrapped around the edge. Granny dragged herself awake and shrank back into the bed, staring at the door as shadowed eyes under blue and orange hair spikes peered from above the fingers. She thought she saw a flash of something: Anger? Defiance? in those eyes, then they were just Alice's eyes, sad and resentful as she pushed the door wide and strode into the room. "Hi, Granny."

"Alice, what are you doing here? Is your mother with you? I thought your mother was coming. Visiting hours don't start until later."

"No. Just me. Mom sent me to see if you needed anything. They let me in for a few minutes because I told them I had to go to the store for you before visiting hours." Alice said, her lips drawn down in what was becoming a perpetual sulk whenever she was around her grandmother. She stared at the teeth in the glass in disgust.

"I need your mother to tell those…those…prison guards, that I'm being robbed!" Granny almost shouted in a whiny, creaky voice.

"She went to Albany. To some conference for the Methodist women," Alice explained. "So. Do you need anything?" She would not even make eye contact with Granny.

"There is a *man*. He comes through that window and he takes my money. My snack money," Granny pleaded. "He thinks I'm asleep. He comes through that window. And. He. Has. A gun."

"Yeah. Mom says that I need to go to the store for you." Alice completely ignored what Granny was saying. "She says you need things like toothpaste and shampoo. I'm supposed to check on those things." Alice went into the bathroom and rummaged in the medicine cabinet. Her voice sounded hollow as she added, "You need new towels and wash cloths? Mom wants to know."

"I don't need *anything*. I just need someone to believe me," Granny said forlornly. "Nobody believes old people."

"So, you only have half a tube of toothpaste. I'll get some and some soap. You just have that little slimy piece. You want any chips or snacks or anything?" Alice started to write a list on old breakfast menu. "Is this what they feed you?" she asked, reading the menu and squinching up her face, repulsed by the offerings.

"It's not so bad. Old people like things bland. Keeps us from being windy. But this man is real." Granny refused to be dissuaded or to have the subject changed.

"If he's real, what does he look like? Why doesn't anyone hear him come in? Don't you have alarms on the windows in this place? Costs enough." Alice blinked in disbelief and resentment. Her mother and Alice had been doing without to keep Granny here.

"They tested the alarms. All in working order. He looks like Bill. He looks like my grandson," Granny broke into tears.

"Bill's been gone for five years. He won't be back. Once he got out of jail, he went west. I think he went to Alaska to work on the pipeline. Last I heard, he was on the run again. He won't come back here. They'd be looking for him," Alice toyed with a little figurine sitting on the nightstand. She hadn't liked her cousin, Bill. He was mean and rotten to the core, although she did think that he might be right about some people needing to be beaten or even killed. She supposed he could have robbed her granny but he was long gone. And Granny was just plain bats.

"I think it's him. It looks like him," Granny said stubbornly. "And he never forgave me for testifying against him when he beat up your Aunt Ellen. He beat her and beat her. I just couldn't stand it anymore. Someone had to stop him."

"Well. I don't think he's here. Maybe. But I don't think so. I'm going to the store. You want anything besides the toothpaste and soap? I can get some of those coconut candies you like so well," Alice offered. Despite being forced to come here every week, she kind of liked the old lady. Even if she was crazier than a Bessie bug.

Granny heaved a sigh, defeated for the moment. "Bring me some of those anti-acids and some baby oil. And some of those red licorice twists. Like those better than the black ones but I'll take the black ones if there isn't anything else. Like to suck on them. I can't pull em apart with my teeth anymore. Have to suck."

"They've got them in little pieces now. They taste the same. I'll get you some of those." Alice said impatiently and wrote it down.

"And some of those coconut bars without the nuts. The dark kind," Granny added as Alice scribbled on the list.

"Got it. And I'll bring you some of that coffee drink you like so much." Alice put the list in her shirt pocket, scowling at her grandmother.

"Not supposed to have coffee but that's okay," Granny's face lit up like a mischievous child.

"Every once in a while won't hurt," Alice quoted her granny, remembering when Granny used to say it while giving Alice milk with coffee and sugar as a child. Those were good times. Sometimes Alice longed for the good times, but mostly she resented Granny for getting old and changing everything. She even found herself wishing Granny would just die so she would not have to be reminded of the good times. So she didn't have to be burdened with a crazy old lady to take care of. "I'll be back in a while. I'll stop at the bookstore and get some of those mysteries you like so much. And a pair of those reading glasses they sell. Yours seem to be broken." She picked up Granny's glasses. The lenses were broken. It looked like someone had stepped on them.

"It was him. They were by my bed, on the nightstand. He knocked them off and stepped on them when he took the money out of my wallet. He thought I was asleep. But I wasn't," Granny said sounding defensive.

"I'll get you some more. I'm off. Be back soon." Alice rolled her eyes about the glasses. Stupid old lady. The she leaned in as if to kiss her, but backed off and left for the store.

The LVNs came in to help her settle for bed, followed by the night nurse who greeted her cheerfully. Granny showed her the broken glasses. The nurse laughed and told her she should be more careful when she got up to go to the bathroom at night. No one listened to old people.

Alice returned just as evening visiting hours started. The sun had set and darkness was building. She had two sacks, one with grocery items and the other with the promised books and two pair of reading glasses. "Just in case," she said darkly.

"What took you so long?" Granny asked, her voice sleepy and cranky at the same time. "Where's your mother?"

"Uh, remember? Mom is busy with the church ladies. So I came." Alice's eyes skittered around the room, finally lighting on the dark window. She wished Granny wasn't so forgetful. Alice sighed as walked over and started to pull the yellowed window curtain aside.

"No! Don't open it!" Granny was pushing herself down into the mattress, trying to get as far from the window as possible.

"What?" Alice turned to her grandmother, dropping the curtain back into place, but not quickly enough. Granny thought she saw something in the window before the curtain dropped. Something that looked shiny-red or slimy-red or maybe just red. Anyhow, whatever she thought she saw was enough to startle a soundless scream from her throat.

Irritated, Alice flipped the curtain open again, watching Granny, her back to the window. "See? Nothing there." Under her breath, she started to mumble, "Crazy old bat…." The end of her sentence was swallowed up when the window exploded in a shower of silvery glass.

A man climbed in through the broken window. He was wearing a red jacket and black pants with bulging pockets. No alarm sounded. There was no noise marking the shattering of glass. The man grinned.

"Why, Alice. How you've grown," he leered. "I put a blanket on the other side of the window. Masks the sound. Only you and Granny here know I'm back. And here. Been playing a little game with her. I been coming in and out of the window while she was sleeping. Silence the alarm and lift the window. Nothing to it. I make just enough noise to wake her and scare the puddin' outta her. Tonight is the final act, I broke through the window this time to really scare her. I've been waiting for a long time for this." He started toward the woman cowering in the bed. "I'll just put my hands around that skinny throat and rip her head off." He relished the thought.

Alice stepped in front of Bill, her back to Granny. "I'll be glad to help you, Bill. All I do is fetch and carry. I *hate* that old biddy," Alice said bitterly.

Bill looked down at Alice, a satisfied gleam in his eyes. "You used to be such a goody two shoes. Look at you now. The little rebel, spikey headed and green fingered." Bill obviously approved. "You sure you can do this?"

"You just give me a gun and watch me." Alice grinned wickedly. She turned around and slapped her granny in the face hard. All the resentment she held for her granny showed on her face.

"Well now." Bill grinned. He picked up the glass and dumped Granny's teeth in his hand. He jammed them into her mouth. "Now you can talk plain, old lady. Now you can tell the police everything. *If* you're still alive to do it." He ground a pair of her new glasses under his heel and laughed.

Alice picked up Granny's frail arm by the wrist. She reached for her medication and popped a pill roughly into Granny's mouth. She jammed a glass of water against her lips and forced Granny to drink long and hard. Granny coughed and sputtered. "Swallow, you old bitty. You want to live don't you?" Alice laughed evilly. "At least long enough to feel the bullet."

"You'll do," Bill said seriously. "You want to get out of this one horse town and come with me? I'm headed to the bank to make a little withdrawal without the slip if you know what I mean."

"I need a pillow and a gun. Gotta take care of Granny here," Alice said grimly and a little triumphantly.

"Well, I got one for each pocket and one for my ankle. Take this one," Bill said. "But I got Granny. I owe her, don't I, Grandma?" he said, passing a gun to Alice and then slowly taking the safety off the one he held in his right hand.

Granny tried to scream but her heart burned and her jaws hurt. Alice moved her hand across the gun, gently caressing it while she slipped off the safety. Bill raised his arm. Alice pulled the trigger and watched Bill fly backward through the broken window.

The door of the room burst open. Nurses flew in and then doctors. Cops were everywhere. An ambulance arrived. Bill would never bother them again.

The next afternoon, Alice's mother sat on the edge of Granny's bed. "I'm okay now," Granny said. "Alice gave me my pill so my heart settled down. They kept me in the hospital a while. But I'm back."

"That Bill was always a bad 'un," her daughter said.

"Ain't never coming back again." Granny nodded soberly. "But my lands, this little one, spikey headed and green fingered, she's the best." Granny took Alice's hand as Alice bent to kiss the top of her granny's head.

"Love you too, Granny," she whispered.

Alexis' Aggravation

Well, there he was dead on the floor of my bar. I've seen dead bodies. I know what they look like all right. The guy just keeled over with a sample bottle of Harry's Best Irish in his hand. And probably down his throat as well. Nice looking corpse. Youngish, handsome...someone I might have been interested in if things hadn't turned out badly for him.

And now the cops are here. You know, I gave that up all that cop stuff. I got tired of all the dead bodies they found when I worked nights in homicide. Owning a quiet little pub across the street from the Convention and Opera House sounded so nice. I even got an antique oak bar from an old speak-easy in Chicago. And now, it's landed in my lap again. This is so aggravating.

"Hey. Alexis, looks like you just can't get away from the bodies, huh?" My former partner, Henrietta, playfully called "Hank" by everyone on the force except me (I hate nicknames) stood up from where she was examining the body.

"Yeah, Alex," (I cringed) another detective, his perfectly tailored Armani suit looking out of place. "I thought you hated all this cop-dead-body stuff. And lookee here, another body turns up on your watch." Marco, my replacement when I quit the force, grinned at me through his perfectly groomed mustache.

"Henrietta, I am so sorry Fancy-Boy Marco is your new partner." OK, that was a nickname, but he's so vain and obnoxious he deserves it! "More to the point, what are you going to do about this? Dead bodies full of booze don't go well with the décor of my nice little pub."

"We're almost finished with the body. Coroner will be wheelin' it out soon. You'll be closed for the rest of today and probably part of the day tomorrow. You know the drill. Sorry." Henrietta was all business. "This will clear itself up soon."

"Better," I said. Business was good but any interruption could be problematic. "But some time off will be nice."

I gave my statement. My work was done, unlike Henrietta's. And Marco's. Marco had always been an after thought. Never liked him. Never would. But I had time on my hands and a ticket to the Alcohol Distiller's Convention across the street. Might as well go over and see what was happening.

I headed for the distributers' booths. Nothing like free samples to perk up my day. It got me in tune with the latest trends in the business and got me away from Marco. Marco wanted me and expected that I wanted him. The convention was a perfect place to hide from his renewed attentions. He creeped me out with his rich boy vibes and frat man attitudes. How and why he ever became a cop was beyond me. I stopped to try the flavored whiskies and forgot about Marco for the moment.

The little sample bottles at the booth reminded me of the bottle the guy that died in my bar was holding. He must have picked it up here before coming to the bar. I wondered what killed him. Probably a heart attack. I did not hear any gunshots and there was no knife poking out of him, no blood. *"Just my luck,"* I sighed to myself. *"Guy with a bad ticker shows up at my bar in time to kick the bucket."*

I started sorting through the various flavors of whisky on display: peach, black cherry, blackberry. *"Who would have ever thought that adding fruit flavors to whiskey would be a good idea?"* Just as I picked out a sample bottle of each, I felt a tap on my shoulder. *"Oh no, Marco found me. Ugh!"* I pretended to smile at him.

"There you are! I thought you took a powder." Marco strutted a bit, showing off his snappy suit and his use of what the thought was equally snappy cop-lingo.

"Now, why would I do that? Henrietta said the bar had to be closed the rest of the day so I thought I would come over here and check out the convention. Bar-tending is my business, after all." I turned back to the whiskey sample display; ignoring Marco, hoping he would disappear.

"Well, thanks for being so accommodating!" Marco grabbed my wrists, pulled them behind me to handcuff them together.

"What?" I turned around, jerking my hands back and saw Marco, dangling a pair of handcuffs and grinning like he just won the lottery.

"Alexis Morton, you are under arrest for the murder of Bobby McGruder." Marco reached for my hands again.

"What? Are you kidding?" I stepped away, thinking it was one of Marco's sick attempts to seduce me.

"Put your left hand on your neck, and your right hand on the table. Now!" Marco barked.

A crowd was gathering as I complied. Henrietta pushed through it, putting a cell phone in her pocket. "Allow me," she said, taking the cuffs from Marco and snapping them gently on my wrists. "You were supposed to let Evans and McRae do this."

She led me through a side door, down a corridor and out to a waiting prowl car, guiding me carefully into the seat. "Sorry. We're officially off the case. Marco wasn't supposed to go near you. We are too close to the main suspect, you, to work on it any longer. Officer Cowan will take you to the precinct. Evans and McRae will do the questioning. Take care of her, Joey."

"Call Mikey will ya and see if he'll make bail?" I asked, hoping my errant brother remembered the favor I did him a couple months ago.

"Already taken care of. Have a good ride." She shut the door and rapped on it. The last I saw of her, she was reaming Marco out big time.

My brother, fortunately for me, was waiting with the bail money after I was questioned, booked and taken down to night court for a brief hearing with Judge Murray. I was afraid I'd never get out on bail. She must have been in a good mood because she only set a $100,000 bond.

"You *are* going to pay me back, right?" Mike asked as he dropped me back at my apartment.

"Yes, I'll pay you back but you still owe me for the pistol I bought you when you joined the Mounties," I replied, exasperated at his lack of trust.

"It is the State Police, not the Mounties. I'm just making sure you remember about the cash part of that bond," he said firmly.

"It's the cute hats. I'll pay the money back already," I said, hugging him, which embarrassed his masculinity. I smiled at his retreating back and shut the door.

"Now, what am I going to do?" I moaned as I leaned against the closed door, "I'm a suspect in a murder!" Just then Charlie and Sassafras came through the kitchen door, meowing loudly as if to say "Where do you think you have been?"

"Oh. Sorry guys, I got hung up a little bit." I headed for the kitchen, their furry bodies winding around my feet, trying their best to trip me. "Hey! If you want me to feed you, you better let me walk."

After I fed the cats, I tried to call my sister, Martha. She was about four years older than me, six years older than Mike, and did not ever hesitate letting us know she was the "big sister." She was also a lawyer. I left a message, telling her I was in trouble and needed her.

The next day, instead of hanging around waiting for Martha to call, I went back over to the convention center. I was intrigued by the flavored whiskey. I fingered the sample bottles and selected three or four. The booth attendant flattered me by checking my ID. I asked if any of the other distilleries were making this. He indicated a very small distillery in the last row of the merchant booths.

"How's business?" I asked of the older man sitting in the booth.

"We're doing pretty well, considering. I've had this business for 57 years. My father and grandfather had it before me. Quality distilling. We make good Irish whiskey the slow way. There is a new fangled method that speeds up the process, but it is pure nonsense. My son and I are still hanging in there with our old fashioned methods. Nobody's run us out of business yet. My son was pretty peeved about it and thought it was the end of us. But we have a good product. Hard to kill a good product," the older man mused.

"I'm Alexis. I own the bar across the street. Sell a lot of your stuff. Drink it myself," I said.

"Well, then you should try this special batch my son made up. He said it was for a friend but he only passed out one bottle. Take it all and pass it out to your customers. See if they like this new flavor he's put added," the old gentleman smiled and passed me a six pack of small bottles minus one.

"Thanks," I smiled at him for being such a nice old man. "I'll try these out. Compare 'em to the ones made by that new process. I'll let you know which tastes better."

"It's the taste and the smoothness that makes Irish whiskey. The golden flow of it all," the old man laughed. "Say, have you heard who is going to give the Keynote speech today? That McGruder fella was scheduled to give it but he got himself killed yesterday. Talk around here is it was poison!"

"Wow, no. I knew about the guy that got killed, but didn't know he was going to give the Keynote. What was he going to talk about?"

"That new-fangled distilling process. Pure nonsense! Humpf." The old man shook his head and turned back to his display, moving the samples around absently.

I put the five tiny bottles in my bag, absorbing this new information, and went to try some other liquors and liqueurs being touted by vendors. The old man's information did make me wonder about things .*"Oh, no, Alexis!"* I told myself. *"You are NOT a cop anymore!"* I decided I'd had enough whiskey samples on an empty stomach, so I went across the street to the pub to see if the crime techs were finished. Martha still had not called.

It was just after noon and the techs had cleaned up and left. The bar was empty, so I went into the small kitchen and fixed a sandwich.

"I heard you made bail," At first I couldn't see who was standing in the doorway; he was in shadow with the sun shining brightly behind him. When he stepped into the bar, I groaned.

"Marco, what are you doing here? Henrietta said you were off the case and not supposed to talk to me, the *main* suspect!" I sarcastically spat out the words.

"Hey, calm down. I'm off duty. I just wanted to make sure you were all right." He seemed a bit edgy. "I was over at the convention, thinking you might be there."

"I was, but came here for something to eat. I don't think I am supposed to talk to you, even if you are off duty. At least, that's what my lawyer said." I crossed my fingers under the edge of the bar because I hadn't spoken to my lawyer yet, but figured that was what she would say.

"Oh? You already have a lawyer? I thought you were *innocent*," he sneered. "Why would an *innocent* person need a lawyer?"

The door opened again; Henrietta walked in. "Marco, what are you doing here?"

Marco climbed on a bar stool, "Having a drink on my day off. What are *you* doing here?"

"Hey, Henrietta, I heard something across the street that might be related to the case," I said, not wanting to share the information with Marco, but also wanting to take the focus off me as a suspect.

"Can I get that drink, please?" Marco looked from me to Henrietta, then back to me. "Now?"

Since I had not set up the bar yet, I pulled a tiny bottle from my bag. "Here, try this. I picked it up from a really nice old man across the street." I grabbed a glass and handed it and the bottle to him. "No charge."

"Wait, who did you say gave this to you?" Marco was staring at the bottle. Was that fear I saw in his eyes?

"Now who?" I said as the door opened once again. "Oh, hello there. Did you come to see my pub?" It was the old man from the distillery booth at the convention.

"Marco?" he asked, "What are you doing here?"

"Dad?" Marco quickly scooped the tiny whiskey bottle off the bar.

"Uh, Oh!" I looked at Henrietta. "About that information I had for you . . ."

"Marco pulled me across the bar by the hair and pointed his pistol at me. "Gotta go. It's been fun. Hank, your gun on the table. NOW!" He let go of my hair; grabbed my bag and the bottles.

"What have you done?" The old man said in bewilderment.

"He was driving us out of business, Dad." Marco whined.

"You shouldn't have done that for me." The old man said quietly.

"I did it for me, Dad," Marco said, "Do you think I want to live on a cop's salary? Move out of the way, Hank."

He backed to the door and stepped out, heading for the curb. A cab pulled up; he opened the door to step in, but backed away. He was surrounded by cops.

Henrietta picked up her gun and sighed. "We suspected him from the start. The security video showed him handing off a bottle to the victim, who had a new method of distilling that took far less time and money than traditional methods. Apparently he wasn't interested in releasing the secret. It would have driven the small distilleries out of business."

"Not ours. We were never in danger. We're one of the oldest distilleries in the US. We have a brand name and we are expensive because we never put out much at a time, but we have a loyal customer base. We're specialty. Our market was not going away. I tried to tell him. He became a cop because he was afraid the business would fail. He just needed to have faith." The old man lowered his head and wept.

Maybe I'll go back to the Force. But maybe not. Seeing the old man weep reminded me that I had helped people doing what I did. I'll just have a drink and think about it. My phone rang. It was Martha.

Mattie's Score

The crowd milled and murmured impatiently outside the Riff-Raff Thrift store while the manager unlocked the inner doors, then slid back the ornate gates. He stood back quickly as the crowd surged forward and swarmed into the store. It was the annual "Rush for Furniture" sale. Pushing and shoving their way into the store, the intrepid shoppers ran to the pieces of furniture that caught their eye. The first customer to touch the furniture won the right to buy it at a discount.

Two men broke out of the crowd and headed toward the back of the store where a lone dilapidated dresser sat with a half-off sign taped to the front. The two men arrived at the same time, slapping their hands on the dusty dresser top.

Charlie Sullivan, the black sheep youngest son of a wealthy family, recognized the dresser from when he was a child. He remembered the scratch he made with an old toy car on the top of it. He could feel the deep scar now in the wood under his hand. Charlie also recalled hiding an old letter in the false bottom of one of the drawers. Since graduating from college and leaving the family home, he had taken up stamp collecting as a hobby. About five years ago, he ran across a picture of a stamp that was quite rare, worth more than Charlie owed the loan sharks he had been trying to avoid.

He was sure the letter he hid in the false bottom of the old family dresser had the same stamp on it. He needed that stamp because he desperately needed the money, having been cut out of the family fortune because of his gambling habits. He had briefly discussed the stamp with a friend in his philatelist club, but no one else knew about it. Or so he thought. He knew his sister was the last in the family to have the dresser and he had been looking for it ever since she died, her possessions auctioned for charity. Now, he finally had his hands on it.

Ed Pickens stood in his way. Ed had been in the antique business most of his life. Since he was a teenager, he had been restoring antique furniture with his father and grandfather. They often ran a con on out of town antique dealers and customers, selling second-rate pieces as the real deal. However, Ed had fallen in love with colonial furniture and this piece, once restored, could become a showpiece in his shop. They could become legitimate or at least run a better con. He recognized the famous colonial designer Fredrick Reynolds' stamp burned on the back of the dresser and knew it would be worth a small fortune in restored condition. "Sorry, bud, I got here first."

"No, I was here first." Charlie responded, "But I tell you what, I'll give you a hundred dollars to get something else."

Ed knew the dresser would make him a lot more than a stack of Benjamins, let alone one, once he restored it. He thought Charlie was an antique dealer new to the area trying to weasel his way into Ed's territory. That would never do. "It's worth a whole lot more than that. What? Do you think I'm an idiot?" He shoved Charlie's hands off the dresser.

"No, no, I was here first." Charlie looked around to see if the clerk heard them. He wondered to himself, "*Did his philatelist friend tell this guy about the stamp? Why else would someone want this old piece of junk so bad?*" He shoved Ed back, "Look, buddy, I tried to be nice, but this dresser is mine."

Ed shoved back, "I'm not your buddy! Don't push me! I was here first! It's mine!" He fired off as Charlie, fists clenched, stepped closer.

"Who do you think you are?" Charlie's now raised voice carried across the back of the store and drew the attention of Mattie Stottlemeyer, an elderly widow. She glanced toward the men, but became transfixed by the dresser that caught her eye just behind them.

It looked just like the one her mother had when she was a child. Mattie remembered her mother telling stories about putting her in one of the drawers to sleep when she was a baby. She also remembered the smell of lavender from the embroidered handkerchiefs her mother kept in the top drawer. She was devastated when a house fire destroyed the old dresser years ago. This was a wonderful find! She waded around the men, who were now rolling on the floor, punching and shouting at each other, her eyes only on the dresser.

The crowd formed a ring around them, blocking both Mattie and the dresser from the men's view. The manager tried to push his way through the crowd. He attempted to get them to stop, and several of the male sales clerks tried to pull them apart to no avail. The manager leaned over the pair, imploring them to stop. A fist knocked him backward into an armoire. The manager rose with help from customers and dabbed his nose with a hankie from his pocket. He pulled out his cell phone, his cultured accent turning to a low Bronx rumble as he called the police.

Meanwhile, Mattie called a female clerk over and quietly paid for the dresser. The police arrived, rushing past a young man loading the dresser into the back of Mattie's car. Mattie dabbed her eyes, feeling warm and loved again as she gazed at the precious dresser. Moving inside, the officers broke up the crowd, handcuffing the two pugilists. Charlie and Ed were shoved unceremoniously into police cars as Mattie drove away completely unaware of the value of the antique dresser or the possibility of a valuable stamp hidden in a false bottom of one of the drawers.

Breakout

"Tell Miss Louisa to smash this bottle and stomp on the ship. What she desires will come to be." The Voodooiene exchanged a burlap wrapped package for Benjamin's small bag of silver coins. "This is a powerful spell, be careful with it."

The next day, Benjamin and Mahala, Lawson plantation slaves for many years, hid the package in one of the empty barrels loaded on the back of the wagon readied for the spring supply trip with the overseer, Mr. Jenkins, and his wife Mary. The three-hour trip brought them to Savannah. While Jenkins and his wife had dinner at a nearby restaurant before returning to the plantation, Mahala and Benjamin visited Miss Louisa at the Savannah Retreat, where the wealthy were committed for mental disturbances.

"I'm not sure I want to see a crazy person, Mahala." Benjamin pulled the package out of the barrel on the back on the wagon and brought it up front as they got ready to leave for the Retreat.

"She isn't crazy, Ben. She's a Northern lady. Her husband, Mr. Jefferson, put her there to keep her from teachin' our kids to read and write and from freein' us all. He knew she would do that while he was gone to war on that big ship." Mahala settled on the wagon seat beside Benjamin. She dug out their travel papers in case the paddy rollers stopped them in the wagon without a white overseer.

"That's a fine ship, that CSS Alabama. The Yanks won't ever catch up with that one." Benjamin slapped the reins on the backs of the matched pair pulling the wagon.

Mahala held on to the wagon seat edge as they pulled out into the street. "Miss Louisa's brother, I believe his name is Franklin Yeats, has been trying to get her out of that place for over two years now. But Mr. Jefferson is the husband and brothers don't have any say in what husbands do to their wives. Maybe after the Yankee Army comes, Mr. Yeats can just take her away with him."

Arriving at the Retreat, Benjamin helped Mahala down from the wagon and held the horses while she knocked at the back door. Mahala explained to the nurse that she had some personal supplies for Louisa Lawson. "She likes it when I fix her hair for her."

"OK, but he will have to stay outside. We don't want no men in here disturbin' the women." The nurse opened the door wide enough for Mahala to enter, scowled at Benjamin and shut the door.

After unlocking and passing through several doors, they found Miss Louisa sitting on the bed, her face turned away. As soon as the nurse left, Mahala placed the package on the bed. "Miss Louisa, we are going to get you out of here." She peeled the burlap and red flannel wrapping off the bottle, and handed it to Miss Louisa. "You have to act like a crazy person. You have to smash the bottle, stomp on the ship inside, yell about Mr. Jefferson leavin' you here in this place. Yell at me, saying you don't want no bottle nor no ship. Then jump on the ship and smash it. All your desires will come to be."

"I'm a Christian woman, I don't believe in this casting of voodoo spells." Louisa looked at the bottle in her hands with distain.

"Just do it, please, Miss Louisa. Just try it. You'll see. Mr. Jefferson won't bother you no more."

Louisa's eyes grew cold and hard at the mention of her husband's name. In a rage, she smashed the bottle on the iron bedstead, and stomped on the ship when it fell to the floor. "There!" she shouted, "Take that for leaving me here, Jefferson!"

A doctor, followed by a nurse, burst through the door at the noise. He held Louisa down on the bed. "Go get the laudanum!" he shouted. The nurse pushed Mahala through to the kitchen, shouting "You! Get out!

Mahala ran to the buckboard where Benjamin was nervously waiting with the horses, who were fidgeting at all the shouting. "What happened? What was all that noise about?"

"Just go! I'll tell you as we head back to Mr. Jenkins." Mahala looked back over her shoulder as the wagon rattled out of the back yard and onto the street.

In early July, as the summer heat started slowing things down, Mr. Jenkins visited Ms. Louisa, telling her the CSS Alabama sank during a battle with the USS Kearsage off the coast of France in late June. Killed during the battle, Jefferson Lawson's body went down with the ship.

Remembering the ship in the bottle, Louisa shrieked with hysterical laughter at the news, and then burst into tears. The nurses calmed her with tincture of laudanum and Mr. Jenkins, appalled at her reaction, decided to leave her at the Retreat until he could locate her relatives.

A few months later, as the leaves started to show fall colors, the nurses discussed the rumors about General Sherman and Yankee Army heading east from New Orleans. They said he was destroying everything in his path and were anxious about what to do with their charges. A huge battle was raging in and around Atlanta in early September. Everyone in Savannah was afraid that Sherman would soon arrive, bringing Yankee destruction with him.

Sherman did arrive just before Christmas, Major Franklin Yeats at his side. Yeats took a detail to the Lawson plantation to find his sister. Jenkins and most of the slaves had deserted the plantation, but Benjamin and Mahala remained, and led Yeats to the Savannah Retreat where Louisa was still confined.

Yeats, his sister, and the two loyal servants continued the march with Sherman and ultimately arrived in Boston. Yeats and Benjamin started a furniture business together, and continued to support Mahala and Louisa, who spent the rest of their lives as suffragists and advocates for the rights of married women.

All that Shimmers . . .

Hank Williams sat behind the casino glass waiting for the woman to pass him her chips. She had the big payoff for the night. He dropped the chips in the slot and listened as the rattled down through the counter. Fifty thousand dollars. He could use 50 thou but it wasn't his. He sighed as he wrote out the check, handed it to the floor manager for her signature under his, then had the winner sign the tax forms before he gave her the check. That was that. He settled back in his chair. Twenty minutes left before the casino closed. He yawned, wishing he was home watching his DVD collection of old sci-fi movies.

The only thing amusing tonight was the Halloween costumes. Everyone was in costume except him and the security men. He'd paid out 10 grand to an old woman dressed as Patience from an old sci-fi series that hadn't gone more than 14 episodes. The costume was pretty awesome, but the old lady wearing it made it look kind of silly. He yawned again and spun his chair around just to keep awake.

There was a flash of light that seemed to move out and then combine again in the middle of the room. He blinked his eyes. Bright blue and purple spots blocked his vision. He rubbed his eyes. Then he brought his hands to his sides and raised them in surrender. A strange figure stood pointing a short metal staff at him.

The staff appeared to be a weapon but Hank wasn't taking any chances. The figure moved. It had three fingers and a thumb on each hand. One eye went round and round in the center of its forehead. Its skin was blue, its lips green. What hair it had was green as well only a lighter shade. Otherwise, it looked fairly human. Two legs. Two arms, a mouth and nose. It made a flute-like query pointing to a tray of cash sitting on a desk.

Hank wasn't sure what it wanted. It gestured impatiently, then mimed a bag. Hank reached over and tossed it a bank bag. The alien began to put the money in the bag.

Hank wondered how it got in the locked room. He moved to press the alarm button but the alien motioned him back with the staff. It must have something to do with that bright light. He moved back. Then he tried moving forward. The alien shot him with a bright laser beam that came from the staff. It burned his arm. Hank yelped, raising his arms again and standing still. The alien went back to putting money into the bag.

Hank looked at his arm. The wound didn't look like anything he'd ever seen before in sci-fi movies. But he realized that he had seen the staff before. Or something like it. It was like a tiny flame thrower. The type you could build in your back yard. Did aliens use flame throwers? He wasn't sure on that.

"So…where're you from?" Hank asked.

The alien looked up. It shook its head. Then it moved to the next tray of cash that Hank had out for counting.

"So…if you're an alien, why do you want money?" Hank mused. The alien paused, then raised the metal rod. "Guess that's your business," Hank shrugged. The alien went back to work on the cash.

The Lone Ranger came to the window to cash in chips. He laughed at the alien. "Good costume." Hank grunted and handed over the chump change for the chips. The alien stood still, holding the rod in his direction. The Lone Ranger left.

As the employees checked their cash in for the evening, Hank expected someone to be suspicious of the alien in the vault room but they were all too tired to care. The change girls took off their heels and headed for the locker room. Only he was left as the security people began locking doors and checking restrooms. The alien began sacking the change girls' money.

"That's about it on the cash," Hank said.

The alien pointed to the wall safe. "I don't have the combination. Night security chief does. He'll be in here soon if you want to wait." The alien fluted some words and pointed the rod at Hank's face. "Or not." Hank moved to the safe and began turning the dials.

As he turned the dials, the thought struck him again. "Why would an alien need money? And how did he know what a safe was?"

The alien moved up closer as the door to the safe opened. The light caught its face. Hank could see a pair of very human green eyes hidden in a mask. He'd been had. Or at least partially had. There was still the question about the bright light and how the so-called alien got into the vault room.

"Hey!" the alien yelled as Hank pushed him onto the floor, then held him there with his knee.

"Ah-ha!" I knew you weren't really an alien! "Now, how did you get into the vault room?"

"Get off me!" The alien squirmed under Hank's knee, rolled out from under it and jumped up, pointing the staff at Hank again.

"Hey buddy, that is not going to work this time. I'm calling security!" Hank reached for the alarm button, but the alien smacked his arm with the staff.

"Wait! I'll tell you what you want to know!" the alien pulled off his mask, revealing an ordinary looking man with brown hair. He looked to be about the same age as Hank.

"I came through a Time Travel Pod," he sighed, pulling his arm out of the costume, his shirt sleeves shimmering under the casino lights.

"Right, a *time machine*," Hank sneered as he tried to touch the shimmery fabric. "What kind of material is that?"

"It's a synthetic Iridium blend. The cheap stuff. I couldn't afford the real thing." The alien finished peeling off his costume, revealing an entire jump-suit kind of outfit made of the shimmery material.

"Iridium! Isn't that a super rare metal?" Hank had stumbled on a page about Iridium when he was surfing the Web one night in boredom.

"Well, in your time, yes. But in the 31st Century we have found out how to mine it and turn it into fabric. All the elders' uniforms are made of it."

"What? 31st Century? Oh yeah, right. You came in a *time machine*." Hank used air quotes showing he did not believe him. "What's your name, anyhow?" The guy seemed harmless enough and Hank was curious about him. He forgot he was supposed to be calling Security.

"Daniels. And I really am from the 31st Century."

"Right. So what do you need money for? Don't they use micro-chips embedded in your hand or something like that in the 31st Century?" Hank could not keep the sarcasm out of his voice.

"That is Science Fiction – the operative word being *Fiction*." Daniels responded. "We still use plain old currency, something I am woefully lacking. Hence the trip back in time to get my hands on some."

"Well, I can't let you take the cash from my trays. I would get in a lot of trouble, not to mention have to pay it back." Hank reached for the bag full of cash. "You are just going to have to *beam* yourself into some other fool's pile of cash." He laughed at his sci-fi joke, missing the bag as Daniels jerked it behind him.

"Um, sorry. I can't leave here. The Time Travel Pod is coming back in…," he looked at an odd compass-like dial hanging around his neck, "About five hundred clicks."

"Clicks?"

"Oh, um, yeah. In your time, I think that is about five minutes." Daniels started wrapping a cord made of some kind of shimmery material, maybe the same as his uniform, through the openings on the leather closure of the canvas cash bag. He stopped suddenly, glanced at the open safe door, and opened the bag again, dropping the cord. "Hurry, put that money in here!"

"No way!" Hank leaned back on the counter, feeling behind him for the silent alarm button just under the edge. "I think I will just wait for your *time machine* to come back!" He found the button and pushed it.

"Oh, ok, I'll leave it behind. I can always come back. I've got enough now to convince the elders that there is lots more where this came from." Daniels glanced at the bag, shrugged, and grabbed a shimmery cord from his pocket. He wrapped it around the top of the bag.

"I don't think you will be coming back real soon." Hank cocked his head toward the sound of running footsteps. He grinned at Daniels. "Security will be real interested in your *time machine* story."

"It's not a time machine, it is a Time Travel Pod, and it's coming right now."

The air started glowing, a bright light flashed, moved in then out again, engulfing Daniels. The light went out, leaving behind blue and purple spots that momentarily blocked Hank's vision. Again.

"What's the problem?" When Hank opened his eyes, two security guards, guns drawn, stood in front of him.

"Uh. Um. Uh." Hank looked around, knowing that nobody would believe him if he tried to tell them about the 'alien' that robbed the casino.

"Hey, where is the cash from your trays?" One guard asked, looking suspiciously at Hank.

"Would you believe someone came from the future and stole it?" Hank asked hopefully.

"Sure, buddy. Whatever you say," the guard grabbed Hank and spun him around, clicking handcuffs on his wrists. "Let's go tell your story to the boss."

As they turned the corner, the light flashed in the vault room again, Daniels stepped out of the glow, bent over and picked up a shimmery cord. The light flashed again and he was gone.

Finding Booth

"John, what are you doing here?" Abigail Winston, lead singer in a quartet whose performances preceded the plays here at Ford's Theater, as she entered the back stage area.

"I would prefer it if you called me JW, please." John said as he hastily pocketed a small pick. "I was just leaving. You're not performing tonight, are you?"

"No, we were told that we weren't needed tonight. I guess the President won't be here before the play starts. I came by to pick up my reticule. You aren't playing in *Our American Cousin* are you?"

"What's that you say? The President isn't coming?" He fingered the pick in his pocket, wondering if the peephole he had just drilled in the door to the President's box was for naught.

"No, I didn't say that. He's going to be late this evening. What do you care? You're not performing are you?" Abigail asked again.

"You're right, I'm not performing tonight. I just came by to make sure everything was set for the actors. It is an important night, what with the President coming and all." Abigail didn't miss the sarcasm in his voice.

"It's no secret you don't like Lincoln, JW. Why do you care what he sees?"

"I don't, really. In fact, I think it is a bit of luck that neither of us will be performing tonight. Now, if you'll excuse me, Miss Abigail, I have an appointment I must keep." JW hurried out the back door. Abigail stared thoughtfully after him.

The next morning, the news was all over the city. The President had been assassinated! At first, Abigail breathed a quick sign of relief when she heard the news - relief that she was not performing last night. Of course, she was horrified for Mrs. Lincoln and hurried over to the theater to find out what had happened.

"You're sure? It was JW?" Abigail remembered the odd conversation she'd had with JW the previous morning. "Poor Lucy! She must be devastated!" Although supposedly a secret, the engagement of JW Booth and Lucy Hale was known throughout the theater community. It was a recent development, but had not been formally announced.

"I'm sure she wasn't aware of JW's feelings about the President." Joseph played the role of Asa in the play. He'd worked with Booth in the past and was well aware of the rancor JW held for the President. Joseph and Abigail were standing beyond the lines of soldiers blocking the theater, away from the crowds circling around, quietly discussing the assassination.

"It's lucky the engagement hadn't been announced, so she should be spared any embarrassment or ill treatment." Abigail didn't mention her encounter with Booth the day before. "Where do you suppose he is? He certainly can't get too far; I heard he broke his leg when he jumped off the balcony onto the stage before making his escape."

"Hasn't been found yet," Joseph said. "I heard that the girl is devastated but she's leaving soon for Spain with her parents. I doubt Booth told her anything. She'd have turned him in were that the case. Or told Robert Lincoln, at least. They're pretty thick."

"I wonder where JW is?" Abigail mused.

At that moment Booth was at the Surratt tavern, gathering his things. He had heard of Mrs. Surratt's arrest and, despite his injured leg, he and his friend, David Herold needed to get away. Herold, after leading Lewis Powell to Secretary Seward's home, now joined Booth in a mad dash to avoid capture.

Booth's leg hurt. He didn't want to stop, fearing Herold would leave him and report Booth's whereabouts to the Cavalry. But Herold talked him into visiting a nearby doctor, a man named Mudd, who set Booth's leg. Herold bragged that Booth had killed the President. Mudd was appalled, making them leave at once, fearing for his own life.

They were turned away everywhere. Booth, who thought he'd be welcomed as a hero, was becoming depressed. No one was willing to risk sheltering him.

"Let's try the old Garrett place," Herold suggested as they rode away from Mudd's establishment.

"We'll need a boat and a guide," Booth decided.

They moved through Maryland, hiding in a pine forest. Herold talked of giving up because the Union cavalry was everywhere. Booth threatened to shoot him if he tried to leave. Herold found some Confederate friends who provided food and a boat. They informed him that one of Booth's friends had been arrested in a small village nearby. He'd talked. Booth became agitated, insisting that they move on.

Herold and Booth took the small boat and rowed across the river without the guide, who refused to go any further. As the river twisted and turned on itself in the inky blackness of night, they lost their way, landing back on the Maryland side. Booth railed at Herold's incompetence but wouldn't let him leave. He knew too much about Booth's plans.

Herold took them across the river at daylight. Booth, angry now and suspicious, took Herold's weapons away from him, making Herold walk in front of him. They reached a home owned by Confederate sympathizers. Surely they would get help there.

Herold knocked on the door, "Greetings, Ma'am. I fear we're a bit early for our appointment with your husband. Might we rest inside while we wait?" She took them to parlor.

Her old hired man told her that these were strangers. He didn't think her husband knew them. He suspected they might be the fugitives the Cavalry was looking for.

Returning to the parlor, she said, "My husband will be back in an hour. It's not proper for a married woman to be alone with two gentlemen in the parlor. I believe that propriety forces me to ask you to leave the house and wait elsewhere."

"Ma'am. We need to rest and eat. My friend's hurt his leg. I'm sure your husband will understand," Herold pleaded.

"My husband's a jealous man. The Garrett farm's just down the road. Only men live there. My servants have packed you food. Good luck on your travels. You'll be most welcome here when my husband returns," she said.

"But, ma'am," Herold pleaded.

"She is right. Propriety is the thing," Booth intervened, afraid Herold would say who they were. He hustled Herold out of the house and down the road.

The woman sent her servant to find the Cavalry. She'd heard rumors of arrests of all who aided the fugitives and she wasn't going to run that risk. Her servant found the cavalry almost immediately, pointing out where the fugitives were.

Garrett didn't want Booth and Herold in the house, but hid them in the barn. He and his boys went about their business, telling Booth to be gone before daylight. Garrett didn't want any Union Cavalry messing around his place.

The Cavalry squad moved through the woods, encircling Garrett's house and barn, materializing quickly in the yard. Garrett greeted them from the porch. It was late at night but Garrett was still dressed.

"Yeah. You can search my place. Ain't nobody here but me. Check the house if you wanna," Garret said.

The soldiers searched the house and outbuildings. They found a young lad hiding in the corn crib. Garrett ran forward. "Don't hurt him. He's my son."

"Where're the men you're hiding?" the lieutenant demanded.

"Ain't nobody here but us," the lad said. "I never mustered of the Confederate army. I thought you was coming to fetch me back."

"War's over. Been over. Where are they hiding?" the lieutenant demanded putting his pistol to the lad's head.

"Over in the barn," the lad caved.

As the cavalry squad surrounded the barn, they heard a heated argument; Herold begging Booth to surrender to save them both.

"We can't get away. They've got us. I don't want to die. Just let me go!" Herold begged.

"We're as good as dead anyhow. Might as well go out fighting for the glorious cause," Booth remonstrated.

"Let me go!" Herold howled.

Booth called out to the lieutenant derisively, "Someone's comin' out." He shoved Herold toward the barn door.

The lieutenant made Herold show his hands. Booth said, "I have all the weapons. I'll be using them on you boys."

Herold ran out of the barn before Booth could shoot him. The lieutenant began negotiating with Booth; hoping he would surrender. Meanwhile, a sergeant started a fire in the back of the barn to drive Booth out. Booth pulled a weapon, ran toward the fire, changed his mind and ran for the barn door. A carbine cracked.

Booth fell forward, a bullet in his brain an inch below the spot where he'd placed one in Lincoln's head.

The lieutenant searched his body. He found a derringer, a compass, a pocket knife, and pictures of five different women. One was Lucy Hale. The rest were actresses.

"Guess all her tears were for nothing," the lieutenant sighed. "The curtain certainly dropped quickly on that romance.

The Gift

A fog hung over the airfield, thick and fat like down pillows. A black stretch limo pulled up to a private cargo jet, small and sleek like the woman standing beside it. She was blond and built, her hair combed neatly in waves down to her shoulder. She wore little makeup, not needing it. Only her lips were deep red to match her long, elegant fingernails.

The limo chauffeur leaped out, opening the back door for a nattily dressed man in a double breasted suit and wing tipped shoes. The man sported a pencil moustache and a self-assured smile. He placed a fedora on his head and almost tapped danced over to the jet. Two large, well-muscled men followed, obviously minions of the man with the wing tipped shoes.

"Hello, Ric. Ready to go?" The woman asked with a slow seductive smile that was more habit than anything else.

"Not yet, Luci. Waiting for Jim. He's coming in his own car with the inventory," Ric said gazing out into the fog. He couldn't see anything. "We flying out in this?" he added, opening a gold cigarette case and passing one to Luci.

Luci nodded and took a cigarette. Ric reached in his pocket for his antique zippo lighter. He looked up to find her cigarette was already lit. Her hands were still on her clipboard and he didn't see a lighter. Her eyes turned a reflective red for a moment as she turned her head into the red lights on the jet wings as they turned on and off. The co-pilot was running the pre-flight tests. "Odd how Luci's eyes changed like that," Ric thought.

Luci interrupted his thoughts. "He the one?" she asked in a bored tone.

"Yeah," Ric said. "ATF. We know but he doesn't know we know. If you get what I mean."

"Here he comes," Luci said, nodding toward the gate to the runway.

A car turned down the lane leading to the jets. It passed the other moored planes, battened down before the incoming storm. The car stopped. The two henchmen, Bub and Damon, went to unload. A man in a subdued suit stepped out, tossing the keys to Bub. The henchmen moved to the trunk to begin loading the cargo. Twenty five sacks of flour this time. Hidden inside were smaller bags of drugs. Bub and Damon handled them like they were empty, carrying stacks of them at a time into the cargo hold of the plane.

The co-pilot stepped down out of the plane. She was a slender, well-built red-head. She nodded to Ric with a slow pouty smile.

"She's ready, Luci," the co-pilot reported, lounging back against the hatch frame, arms crossed, waiting.

"Luci, Chris, this is Jim Moore, my number one," Ric made the introductions grandly, gesturing with a flourish to Jim, the man in the subdued suit. "Jim, pilot Luci Fiera and co-pilot Chris Satana. They've been ferrying me around for a while. Good pilots. Know how to keep their mouths shut." Ric's words were bitten off and hard with the last sentence. He eyed Jim coldly and then broke into a smile. "Like you." Ric added.

Chris smiled at Jim, extending a hand. Luci laughed at Ric's jest and then welcomed Jim aboard. The henchmen were finished loading. Not a hair out of place and not one speck of flour or anything else dotted their suits. "You know Bub and Damon," Ric added. The men nodded.

"It's loaded, Mr. Allman," Damon reported to Ric. Ric nodded and motioned for everyone to board.

Ric boarded the plane followed by Jim and the henchmen. Luci shrugged at Chris, whose eyes looked a bit strange for a second, the pupils almost elongated. Luci laughed quietly to herself. They brought the rear ramp up, boarded through the passenger hatch and headed for the cockpit. Chris stopped to plant a light kiss on Jim's mouth. Her eyes glowed a little red in the light of the emergency door lights. Jim sat back in surprise.

"Last rites," she smiled sweetly. Then seeing Jim's discomfiture, she added, "Before flying. New man on the plane always gets a peck just before we take off. Last rites." She grinned and took her seat. "Buckle up, boys. Maybe a little rough. Airsick bags are in the right-hand pocket of your seats."

Jim was disconcerted about the last rites thing. He tried not to show it but it was just him against the world here. Did they know? If they did, he was a dead man and he knew it. He grinned at the kiss hoping no one had noticed his flinch. The red eyes thing put him off. Was it just a reflection of the lights or was she just a strange girl? He needed to be awake and alert. He started to sweat a little and, once the plane was in the air, got up to use the restroom to recover his equilibrium.

"Better let me check the john for rats, Mr. Moore," Bub said moving to intercept him. The words were like stainless steel in a steel drum. His eyes were hostile. Jim stopped. Bub gave a laugh and the others joined in. "Got ya, Mr. Moore. Got ya." Bub smiled warmly and let Jim pass. Jim joined in the laughter, closing the door behind him.

The plane bucked a little under his feet. He grabbed the sink to steady himself. They knew. He was going to have to think of a way out. That wasn't going to be easy. They were flying at a lower altitude, though, trying to stay under the radar. Maybe he could get a parachute. A parachute would do the trick. He washed his hands and dried them carefully. He'd act scared about the storm. He'd act scared and put on a parachute. It might work.

He opened the door of the restroom and stepped out. Damon steadied him as the plane shimmied a little, his meaty hand on Jim's back. Jim looked out the windows. It was raining now, heavily. Lightning was flashing outside the plane. He shivered. Maybe he didn't have to pretend.

"Ric, don't you think we should find somewhere to set this baby down?" Jim asked.

"Storm getting to ya, Jim?" Ric smiled smugly. "Got the best pilots in the world. They can fly anywhere, anytime. Regular Amelia Earharts."

"It's the lightning. I didn't think it was safe to fly in lightning." Jim shivered involuntarily as a bolt came close to the plane.

"Flown in worse. Luci never lets any of them hit the plane. Right, Luci?" Ric laughed scornfully at Jim's obvious distress.

"Nope. Never will. I like flying in this kind of weather. Wild and fun. Nobody else up here but us." Luci said with satisfaction. Her eyes danced on the edge of wildness, her long red fingernails tapping on the yoke resembled talons in the dim light. Jim almost expected her to turn into a werewolf and howl.

"I'm getting a parachute on," he said. "If that doesn't bother anyone else."

"Take one out of the drawer there. Best parachutes money can buy. Make the packers jump everyday with one of the ones they packed. No one's died yet." Ric grinned at Chris, whose co-pilot seat was just behind his. He pulled out the cigarette case and chose one. He stuck it in his mouth. He grinned at Chris again. His cigarette lit on its own. Ric pulled it out of his mouth and stared at it. Chris' eyes glowed faintly of red. She turned back to the controls.

"Better fasten your seatbelts. It's getting rough out there," Chris suggested.

Bub and Damon turned their seats so they faced each other and pulled trays out of the arms, twisting them so they covered their laps and formed a table between them. Bub drew a pack of cards from his shirt pocket and dealt a hand to each of them. The quiet slapping of the cards served to calm Jim's nerves a bit, but he glanced at Ric, wondered just exactly what he knew. He settled the parachute straps over his shoulders, buckled it across his chest, and sat back down.

"Hey Jim," Ric leaned forward, fastening his seatbelt and tapping his cigarette ash on the floor. "How's yer sister? Last I heard from you, she was having some problems with her *pregnancy*." He stared right at Jim while emphasizing the last word.

Jim didn't have a sister, but he had told Ric he did to cover his absence over the previous weekend when he was filing his report with his ATF handler. "Um, yeah, she's fine." Jim was really sweating now. "It turned out to be a false alarm."

"That's good. Wouldn't want anything *bad* to happen to her, now would we?" Ric stubbed his cigarette in the ashtray built into the arm of his seat.

A guttural growl from the direction of the two card-playing henchmen caught Jim's attention and he glanced sharply toward them. "What was that?"

Ric jumped at the sound and stared at his two minions. "Yeah…"

"Sorry, boss." Bub offered, "Just clearing my throat, didn't mean to scare ya."

Ric shrugged, and turned back to Jim, who had gotten up and was making his way slowly toward the passenger hatch. "Where do you think you're going?"

"Just stretching my legs. I get cramped up sitting in airplanes." Jim glanced nervously toward the hatch door. "*I wonder how hard it is to open that thing,*" he thought to himself. He had to get out of this plane. Ric would not hesitate to kill him if he even thought he was an agent, and Jim suspected that Ric knew.

"Um, did you get the contact information for when we get to Philly?" Jim tried to get the conversation off him and on to the reason they were flying through this storm to Philadelphia. Before they left, Ric had complained that he wasn't sure yet who they were meeting and he did not like 'flying blind' into a situation with such a big load of inventory.

"Nah, I checked my phone just before we got on the plane. Nothing." Ric did not seem too upset about not having the information, but he did look at Jim thoughtfully for a while before saying, "What difference does it make to you? You're not making the drop."

"Just making conversation. I'm a nervous flyer, in case you hadn't noticed." Jim wanted to excuse his obviously increasing unease. He didn't want Ric to know that he knew that Ric knew. He was right in front of the hatch – all he needed to do was grab for the handle, wrench it open and jump out. And hope the parachute opened.

Up in the cockpit, Luci and Chris glanced at each other, eyes flashing red; pupils nearly shut forming vertical lines in the bloody irises. They shared a grin, blinked and looked out at the lightning flashes with normal eyes. Both of them looked a bit smug when they saw Ric's startled face reflected in the dark glass.

Ric leaned back in his seat, certain that what looked like reflections of red eyes with long pupils in the cockpit window was a trick of the storm and the lightning. "Well," he cleared his own throat with a sound not nearly as guttural as what Bub had made, "Jim, why don't you sit back down and we will go over the plan." He started to rise with the seatbelt still fastened, reaching toward Jim.

Jim grabbed the latch, jerked it up, and the hatch door flew open; the momentum and outburst of air drug him through the opening. He hung onto the latch for a second or two, then let go, scrambling for the rip cord on the parachute.

"It won't do him any good, that chute won't open." Luci said as she and Chris turned their seats around.

Ric sat back, the seatbelt still holding him in, and laughed. "Well, that was easy." He grinned at Luci and Chris.

"Make 'em scared enough and they'll do anything," Luci said as the others laughed. "Time to pay up, Mr. Allman. We did as you asked and you promised us anything we wanted."

"Want the plane? She's a good ship," Ric said. "Brand new. Got the title right here in Damon's briefcase."

"We don't own *things*," Chris was disdainful. "We own *people*."

"Nobody owns me," Ric said belligerently. "Take it or leave it."

Luci rose from her seat. "Mr. Allman, you promised us anything. We're not in the business of property. We're in the business of souls."

Ric burst out laughing. "Souls? That's funny. I don't think I even *have* a soul."

"I beg to differ, Mr. Allman. You did say anything. And that's all we want," Chris said.

Ric reached in his pocket and pulled a pistol out. He pointed it at Luci. Her pupils elongated in the bloody irises, eyes shooting out a steady beam of red energy. The pistol went flying from his hand.

"Mr. Allman, my name is Luci Fiera, daughter of Luther Fiera or, as you call him, Lucifer." Luci seemed to grown in stature. Her fingernails grew into red talons. Two small horns emerged from her brow. Her boots split off, revealing cloven hooves. "And this is my cousin, Chris Satana, daughter of my uncle Satan." Chris now transformed looking much like Luci, only shorter. "It's time. We'd like your soul as soon as possible. We have a quota. Time is a factor here," she added in a matter of fact tone almost as a lawyer would negotiate terms.

"No. No! Ric tugged frantically at his seatbelt. You can't take my soul. You can't. Boys, kill them." Ric turned to Damon and Bub pointing at Luci and Chris but to no avail. The two men shimmered. Before him now stood two large salivating creatures with huge canine teeth and long sharp claws. The Hounds of Hell advanced upon him. Damon reached out a set of claws to impale Ric.

The seatbelt buckle finally opened and Ric barely escaped the claws, leaping out of his chair and diving for the cabin wall. He screamed as the jet stream caught him, dragging him along the wall as he frantically grasped objects that failed to stop his slow progress to the open hatchway. He hung on to the hatch frame in one last attempt to remain in the plane, his pleading face on Chris. She smiled and blew him a kiss just before his grip loosened and he fell from the plane.

"That was easy, "Chris said.

"Make 'em scared enough and they'll do anything," Luci said as they all laughed.

Chris inhaled in the direction of the hatch and then exhaled into a small box. A yellow light emanated inside it as she closed the box. "Goodbye, Ric," she said sweetly. "Dad is going to like this present very much."

Shipwreck

The forecast called for high clouds, soft breezes, and mild temperatures. A perfect day for a picnic at the old lighthouse. After filling my dad's sailboat with blankets and a basket of food and drink, the four of us, fast friends our whole life, sailed at daybreak. One last adventure. We moored at the old dock and headed up to sit on the slight hill to the east of the old lighthouse, watching the little waves splash over the rocks below while we ate our lunch. We talked boys, college, and the changes coming to our lives as we prepared to graduate in a couple of weeks.

The temperature dropped. We put on windbreakers and started packing. Stowing the gear below, we did not notice the clouds boiling up over the ocean, black and green, until it was too late. The squall hit hard with unexpected ferocity unleashing torrential rain. Waves dashed against the boat. Lightning split the sky, silhouetting the old lighthouse against the dark clouds. The wind and waves were too high to take the boat out. We ran for the lighthouse with blankets and a basket of food and water, aware of the grave danger we were in, trapped on the island. Over the noise of the thunder and wind, we heard a crackling voice coming from inside the basket.

"What's that?" Mona jerked the lid open, half expecting to see something unworldly cackling through the storm.

"It's the walkie-talkie – my dad insisted we take it in case there was a storm and our phones didn't work." Sally grabbed it from the basket.

"Good thing. I don't have any bars," Sharon raised her phone above her head, squinting at it through the growing gloom as she pushed the lighthouse door open with her foot.

"Small craft warning. Sit out the storm. Stay on high ground." The walkie-talkie squawked. We crowded into the lighthouse doorway. The rain blew in. We moved inside and gazed out the window as the wind really picked up. Lightning was striking all around.

"Is that a ship out there?" Sally rubbed the fog off one of the windows and pointed out to the roiling ocean below the lighthouse. "We need to turn the lighthouse lamp on so they don't run into the rocks!"

"There's no power out here on the island! Not for years!" Sharon shouted between thunderclaps.

"Let's start a bonfire! We've got to warn them!" Mona ran out to drag pieces of driftwood off the beach. The lightning drove her back in. "It's so wet, I don't know if we can get it going anyway," she wailed. We tried to start a fire with the saturated wood in the fireplace, but were only able to generate a few wisps of smoke and a tiny flame.

"It's not going to be any better down at the beach," I yelled over the wind.

A huge grinding, crashing noise startled us. We looked up from our wet, smoky fire and ran to the windows see the ship smash into the rocks below the lighthouse. We watched in horror as people started abandoning the broken ship, some in lifeboats and some just jumping into the crushing waves. The lifeboats capsized immediately, throwing the people into the churning sea. We ran down to the beach through the lightning and rain to help.

The screams of drowning people echoed through the wind, punctuated by huge claps of thunder. We helplessly watched as, one by one, the people disappeared under the water and did not come back up.

"We have to help them!" Mona shouted.

"How? We'll drown if we go into the water! We can't take the boat out. It's too rough!" Sharon yelled in her ear, holding her back from plunging in.

The walkie-talkie crackled again. "Help us! Help us! We can see you. Get help!" A man's voice begged. We could see him frantically signaling with a lantern. The ship rose high on the rocks and sat back down hard. The screams began again as people fell from the ship. They swam toward us but the waves picked them up and dashed them against the boulders.

Fog rolled in as the rain stopped. We could hear moaning start up from the beach. It was coming toward us, eerie and long. It repeated, louder. Mona wanted to stay to help whatever it was. The rest of us ran, hustling her along with us. Sharon slammed the door of the lighthouse, putting the heavy bar in its slot on the door with Sally's help.

I found some old timbers under a tarp and got the fire blazing. We huddled together, back to back, as the moaning rose around the lighthouse. We could see figures moving outside the windows that rattled as people, kelp-draped and water-bloated with cloudy, staring eyes, banged on them. The door visibly shook from the battering. We were too scared to move. I heaped more wood on the fire. The fog was so thick that we could see nothing. The moaning continued, growing more distant.

None of us slept, just stoked the fire and hoped for sunrise. At last, the sunlight arrived. The storm passed. Sharon poked her head out first, the rest of us cautiously following. Then we realized Mona was missing. There were footprints in the wet mud, heading down to the empty beach. There was no ship. No bodies. No debris. Nothing to indicate the shipwreck in the night.

We ran for the sailboat for help, calling for Mona. She didn't answer. Sally untied the mooring ropes and jumped aboard as I started the engine and pulled out, not bothering with sails. We made it back to tell the story, but no one ever found a trace of Mona.

Old timers didn't know of any shipwreck near the lighthouse and the library produced no records, not even in the lighthouse keepers' logs. We never went back. Ever. We weren't pushing our luck by going back. We rarely talked about it.

Unexpected Love

Dust settled in the tracks made by my sneakers as I wound up the road to the statue, my heart heavy despite the chocolate donut in my hand.

Dressed in civil war attire, the statue stood with rifle in hand guarding the cemetery. Most of the men buried here were from the civil war era so it's fitting he guards them. My husband Dan is not buried here; he was a soldier of another era. His body lies lost somewhere in Vietnam.

I come most Saturday mornings to be near the dead, somehow feeling closer to Dan. I always bring a chocolate donut and leave it by the statue's left foot, an offering to a man who loved chocolate donuts almost as much as he loved me. I never knew what happened to the donut after I left. I didn't care. I liked to think that it showed Dan that I missed him.

"You should leave coffee, too." A male voice joked behind me.

I jumped and turned. It was early. I thought was alone here. The young man who joined me wore a wool overcoat against the fall chill. The hat in his gloved hand and the boots he wore suggested he was some kind of workman.

"Sorry I scared you. Seen you here before but it's the first time I've had a chance to talk. Everyone calls me Billy." He nodded.

"My name's Ruth. My husband died in Vietnam. I come up here to be near him." I warmed to the young man.

"Where's he buried?" he inquired looking about.

"I don't know. Somewhere in Nam, I guess."

"That happens in war. The widows left to mourn never knowing a fellow's fate." Billy nodded. "Knew a young man whose wife just got his body delivered to her. Never knew anything more. She died grievin'. When that happens, a body feels guilty and it's hard to go on. You can't meet up in the hereafter, I don't think, with all that grief and guilt blocking things. It's sad for 'em."

"I think if you love someone, you never get over their loss." I sat down on the bench next to the statute.

"There's no getting over the loss but there is being at peace with it. The dead don't like it when their loved ones don't move on. Makes 'em feel guilty for leaving and then guilty because the still living don't make something of their selves. Everyone has a fate. Nobody likes to think he held anyone back just 'cause he died." Billy crushed his cap harder in one hand and then twisted it with the other hand.

"I never thought of it like that. My husband and I came up here on our first date. Memorial Day. The town decorated the cemetery with flowers. There was a big picnic and concert. It was lovely day. Dan kissed me right here. He left his donut on the statue when we went to eat." I reminisced.

"So you come up here to remember that day?" Billy asked.

"I suppose. I miss him. I've done things. Traveled. Taught school. Raised a child he never saw. But never remarried. There wasn't anyone like him, "I explained sadly.

"My wife was a school marm," Billy remembered. "She died. She loved children. We never had any."

"I'm sorry. I've been caught up in myself, I guess. Others have their own grief."

"Everyone has grief. Dan's beside himself that you never found another fellow," he said. "It's not too late. That handyman sure took a shine to you."

"What? How do you know?" Hank had been my handyman for years, helping me keep the house up. I'd never allowed him to be a possibility.

"People talk. They never think I hear. But I do. You take my word. He talks to his boy over there who drowned. Boy's gone on but Hank thinks he's there." Billy pointed toward a row of graves.

"Nobody wants to be left behind," I thought aloud.

"I've got to get. People coming. I want you to know you helped me. I understand my wife better. Think I'll see about finding her. You take care. Here comes Hank." Billy nodded to the road.

I watched as Hank turned down a row of graves. I knew his wife and son were buried here but I'd never asked where.

"Do you think that he would mind me joining him?" I asked.

"Naw." Billy encouraged.

I walked down the row of graves. Hank was arranging bachelor buttons on his son's grave. Roses were neatly arranged on his wife.

"Hi," I said, "Do you think your wife minds me joining you?"

"She told me to find you," he said simply.

"She told you? How…?" I glanced around, listening for — something.

"If you open your heart, you hear them," Hank said.

He reached for my hand as we left, then pulled back. I stopped so suddenly that Hank stumbled.

"What's wrong?" he asked, glancing at his empty hand.

I pointed at a grave marker.

"Billy Miller? He was a Yankee. Killed at 19. His wife grieved until she caught fever and died. Her folks never liked him so she's up in Aspendale. It's a family legend, she was my great-aunt." Hank frowned. "I always thought someone should move one body or the other so they'd be together."

"Can't something be done now?"

"It's an idea. Maybe. But for now, we need to let the spirits move about. It's All Saints Day. They've visiting to do."

People called it a whirlwind romance but we'd known each other too long. I was so blind I just hadn't seen it. We were married in the spring.

Hank, true to his word, had Billy's wife reinterred next to Billy. We planted flowers on their graves. I looked back after we finished. Sure enough, Billy and his wife stood waving to me, Dan next to them eating a chocolate donut. He was happy and I was finally at peace.

Video Games

The wind blustered its way around the house as Delores Castro dug in her jacket for the house key. She took her glove off and dug further into her pocket until the cold keys stung her hand. She shivered as she found the right key and pushed it into the lock, opening the front door.

"Mr. Albertson? Mr. Albertson?" Her voice echoed down the corridor. There was no reply.

There was a note on the phone table addressed to her. It detailed what Mr. Albertson wanted to be done by his housekeeper. He had gone to work to test out his new video game. The heat was on. She could regulate the heat if she wished. Lunch was in the fridge.

She sighed. He almost never was home anymore when she came. He was a good man. One that she…well. She was only the housekeeper, anyway. She started working, cleaning the kitchen and the front room, changing sheets and picking up stray socks that went into the laundry basket with the other dirty clothes.

She carried the basket down the hall toward the laundry room, stopping at his office. The door was open which was unusual. Setting the basket down, Dolores poked her head inside. What a rat's nest! She eyed the video game console sitting on the desk along with many illustrations of game characters and scenes, scripts that were marked, corrected and changed. Daniel must have forgotten to unplug it. It was glowing, beckoning her with the soft pulsing lights but she had work to do. It had been over a week since she cleaned it.

Maybe she ought to just unplug the console. She turned her head, listening. Was that a humming sound? Dolores had never heard that before. She wiped her hands down the front of her thighs, straightening the already straight uniform. Why Daniel insisted she wear a uniform when she cleaned was beyond her. She was just a housekeeper, after all, not a maid!

"What's going on?" Dolores whispered. She glanced around, seeking the source of the humming. Was it the video game console?

She touched the console, turning it so that she could see the controls. It whirred. She touched the keyboard to turn the console off. A green light emitted from the machine. Delores vanished, the laundry basket the only evidence that she had been there.

"I wonder why Delores is still here." Daniel thought as he drove into the driveway after work, noticing Delores' faded blue Honda parked at the curb. He punched the remote garage door opener and waited as the door cranked up. He drove in and entered the house as the garage door lowered.

"That's odd," Daniel muttered as he went through the laundry room. There was a strange, muffled humming sound. "Delores? What is that sound?"

He moved on through the kitchen, expecting to see his housekeeper any moment. There was no noise other than the low humming sound. It appeared to be coming from his office. *"Maybe she's running the vacuum in there."* He pushed the already open door open further and was surprised to see the office empty as well.

"Oof! What's this doing here?" The full laundry basket barely moved when he stumbled into it. He reached for the desk to steady himself, bumping the keyboard with his hand. A green light shot out from the keyboard. Daniel vanished.

He was lying flat on his back when he woke. The first thing he saw when he opened his eyes was … nothing. Just endless black, pierced with occasional red, green, yellow, and blue light flashes. He rolled over, pushed himself to his feet and then fell back to his knees. He could see nothing. There was obviously a floor, he was kneeling on it, but there was no beginning or end to the black. Those light flashes were the only thing keeping him from drowning in the black.

A keening started to his right, weak at first but getting louder. Eerie, but familiar. "Who's there?" he demanded.

The keening stopped. "Mr. Albertson?" a voice asked. "What happened? Why are the lights off? What are those flashes?"

"Delores?" Daniel recognized her voice. "Where are we?" He felt something brush up against the hand he held out, reaching toward the snuffling sounds.

"Turn on the lights, please. I'm scared." Delores implored, running her hand up his arm, fingers flickering on his face. "What is that? Mr. Albertson, what's on your face?"

"What do you mean? There's nothing on…whoa! Where did this come from?" Daniel's fingers touched his face meeting some kind of mask. He explored further, discovering a sharp vertical ridge running from his nose up to the top of his head, where it ended in a spike. His cheeks felt like leather, swooping out at the ears. He tugged but it was part of him, not a mask.

"Delores, check your face. It's different, too." He could see her face reflected as the colored lights flashed again.

"What is this? How did this happen? I can see you now in the flashes. You, you … look like the sketches on your desk. I remember now. There was a green flash. Then everything went black." Delores looked down at her hands and saw long, tapering fingers – six of them on each hand.

"I can't believe this! It's impossible." Daniel's six-fingered hands continued to explore his head and body. "Look. This is a uniform. And you are right, it *is* exactly what I was drawing on the avatars in my newest game."

"Mr. Albertson?" Delores looked at Daniel, "What happened?"

"Call me Daniel. … I think we're together inside my video game."

"What? How…? I don't understand." Delores sighed and sat down on a chair that just seemed to appear when she needed it.

"I'm not sure how it happened, but if I'm right, we need to get out the game quickly. I can't quite explain it, but if we can find the exit, we need to do it fast."

"OK, are we in danger? There's nothing here but us and this chair." Delores patted the chair under her.

"Well, for one thing, we need to find someplace with some light so we can see where we are. Come on, take my hand. Let's start walking, there must be a wall somewhere – we just can't see it because of the black," Daniel instructed.

Delores gladly took his hand, something she had thought about often before this predicament. They walked together, their free arms stretched in front of them, searching for something solid. It didn't take long. They bumped into a wall and started running both their hands all over it, looking for anything that could help them.

"Here! I think I found it," Daniel almost shouted in relief. "There is a button here. Hold on to my hand. I am going to push it and whatever happens, I don't want us to get separated." She took his hand again, closing her eyes.

"That's better. Wow! That was a *really* bright light," Daniel almost laughed. "Are you all right?"

"I had my eyes closed. I didn't see anything," Delores opened her eyes. "What is this?"

She gazed out on a room with gold walls encrusted with jewels. They were on a dais at the end of the room, a large bronze chair draped in velvet of many shades of purple moved to her rear as she walked. She sat down.

Tall figures with faces like Daniel's entered the room. They posed near the doors, weapons raised as if in salute. Trumpets sounded. Smaller figures came through the doors and took seats below her. Their eyes gleamed in leather-like faces, ears swooping majestically to the top of their heads.

Two of the tall figures approached, one with documents on a tray, one with a small lap desk. They bowed, placing the tray on the desk before placing it on her lap.

"Goddess: Please read these appeals from your humble servants and write your portents on these sheaves so that they will know your answers," the figure holding the desk pronounced.

Delores' mouth flew open. She started to rise in surprise, to protest, to deny that she was anything but a lowly housekeeper trapped in a world that was increasingly more confusing. Before she could do anything, Daniel stepped forward.

"Hannakai. Please. A moment for your intended." Daniel said. The smaller figures rose. "In private, please." Delores motioned and they sat back down in unison. "Thank you, Hannakai, for your patience." She rose and followed him to a small room behind the dais. One small figure trailed behind.

"The Chaperone." Daniel explained in a whisper as they walked. "Listen to me. "You are Hannakai, Goddess of the Harakons. You are the leader of these people. I am your second cousin, Rakanabi. Your intended. Follow my lead."

Delores nodded, smiling slightly to herself. They entered the chamber followed by the Chaperone, who sat quietly down on a stool in the rear of the room away from the couple.

"The barbarian invaders will attack very soon. We must leave here so that we can figure out how to get out of here. We must go now." Daniel said in low tones. "There is a traitor in our midst."

"Who? Who would risk defying a goddess?" Delores asked remembering the folk tales of her youth about hubris and the revenge of the gods. "And how do you know these things?"

"I'm not sure. In the script, it was one of the ladies in waiting. Not her." He indicated the Chaperone with a slight inclination of his head.

"The SCRIPT?" Delores was incredulous. "What script? This is real life here."

"It's my video game," Daniel protested.

"No. It's my life. It's what I've always wanted to be. A goddess. Not some cleaning lady that no one ever notices." She was angry, bitter and mad at herself for saying what she always wanted to say to him. "I always wanted a hero."

"Well, that's not me. I'm just a nerd who makes video games that don't sell very well. They're too romantic. The guys don't like them. They just want war and violence and gathering up the spoils." He sighed.

"I love your games. And I'm going to save these people. They're supposed to be *my* people. So I guess it's up to me," she said firmly.

"We have to get out of this game before we're destroyed. I tell you, we *will* be destroyed. I wrote the script," Daniel urged.

"Then we defeat the computer. We change the game," she said defiantly.

Delores turned on her heel and marched back into the throne room, disappointed in Daniel. The chair followed her. She pointed to a spot on the floor imperiously. "Stay," she commanded. The chair stayed.

Striking a majestic pose, she called her troops and generals out, urging them to take courage and heart. She outlined her strategy to stop the barbarians, counseled her troops and her generals to hold firm. Then she commanded them to bring a horse. She headed out, not waiting for her troops to follow. They gathered their forces and hastened behind her.

She rode towards the mountain pass the barbarians would have to take if they wanted to invade her lands. She abandoned her horse to move on foot when the trail became narrow and too rocky for him to travel further. The moon lit her way. Soon, she came to the other side of the pass, searching for the enemy encampment.

The crescent moon shone above the horizon. She saw the enemy pickets and the campfires of the enemy troops ahead. She unslung her crossbow from her back and cranked it tight. Loading her arrow, she aimed it at the pickets. A sharp twang and a succeeding wail of anguish indicated a successful shot. "Wow. My character is a pretty good shot," she said. "I'm a pretty good shot," she corrected, cranking the bow taut and adding another arrow. She caught another of the pickets and the game was afoot.

Alarm spread through the enemy camp. Foot soldiers ran for their weapons and troopers ran to catch their horses. Delores drew her long sword and streaked for the pass. "Whoa. I can really run," she said aloud, amazed at her new abilities. "Wonder if I can use this thing," she added glancing at the sword as she ran.

The horsemen arrived first. They were grinning with the thought of easy rape and kill. They circled her until she backed against the wall of the pass. Then they dismounted and headed confidently for her. She raised her sword, laughing with the pleasure of the coming battle.

Her blade rang as she swung it against the blows of the enemy. She was taking them two at a time, thrusting, parrying and striking with deadly force. More were coming. She had to finish this quickly, and continue into the pass, drawing the enemy in with her.

She heard the sound of hoof beats. A white horse, fire in his eyes, mane flying, and ears laid back swept past her, the heads of the last two attackers bouncing across the trail in its wake. The rider turned the horse and swept her up behind him as they raced back into the pass, heading to the their homeland. It was Daniel, her hero.

Hannakai's troops, who lay in quiet ambush, swooped down to surround the enemy as they swarmed unaware into the pass. The enemy was easily defeated. The homeland was safe. Their goddess was safe. The troops blocked the pass, many remaining to stand guard while the rest returned home in cautious triumph.

Hannakai rewarded her troops with medals and a feast. She sat with her intended, Daniel, at the feast table. "Have you found the way back?" she asked Daniel.

"Yes. I can introduce a virus from the tablet I carried when I was transported." He pointed to his tablet on the table. "It will destroy the program. We can transport safely back then, as long as we are quick."

"I don't wish to return. I don't want to go back to housekeeping. I like what I am here, this body, and its power. Can you go back without me?" she inquired.

"I could. But I don't want to. I have always loved you, ever since that day that you made me stop what I was doing and put that nest of baby birds back into the tree from where the wind had blown it. I knew I loved you then," he replied.

"Why didn't you ever say anything?" she asked aghast.

"I didn't think you'd love a nerd like me," he stated simply.

"I loved your games. How could I not love their creator?" She smiled crookedly at him.

"If you stay, I stay," he said decisively.

"You are my intended, Rakanabi," she answered kissing him.

The game console slept, the laundry forgotten. The house sat, waiting.

Hooked

Ros stood at the counter looking out at the wet night and then gazed around the small coffee house. Not one soul out on this wet, rainy night in this podunk little town.

"Close this joint up," she quietly and then more firmly, "Turn the sign around, lock the door and close this joint up." She strode to the door locked it and flipped the sign over.

"We gonna get in trouble?" Norah, the round little cook asked, looking up from her baking. She deftly turned her fried pies over and held the turner up as she asked, surprised that Ros was closing early. Ros never closed early. 9 P.M. on the dot every night.

"It'll be all right, Norah. I'll tell the owners nobody wanted to come out in this hurricane." Rosalind crossed her fingers behind her back. *"Let this be the last time I have to close this place down,"* the thought ran silently through her head.

"Hurricane? *Hurricane?"* Norah belly laughed. "This little drizzle? Baby, you ain't never *seen* no hurricane if you think this here is one. I'm from New Orleans. This is just a whisper. What's gotten into you? Closing the shop early. That's not you, baby."

"Aw, it's this town. It's my life. It's…" Ros's voice dropped off as she gazed out the window at the dead end town she lived in. Her eyes turned to the patched up booths with seats crushed by too many butts, the antique cash register, the mismatched plates and cups in the bus boxes. She inhaled deeply, catching the scent of fried pies and stale coffee. Her sigh pushed her back to leaning against the counter.

"You just got the blues," Norah said lifting out her pies from the hot grease. "It's that Ralph. What you doing with a guy like that. No brains." She patted the little pies down with a paper towel to catch the extra grease. "Nice boy but nope. Not a lick of sense when it comes to girlfriends."

"He's okay. It's just … well. He came in here last Friday and I was all dressed up for the date he said was going to be somewhere fabulous, but instead he took me out in the country. We went out in the country in the soft moonlight where no one else was and we stopped. And we talked. And I thought it was going so well. Then five guys showed up with their girlfriends and we went cow tipping. *Cow Tipping!*"

"Ain't nobody able to tip them things over. They heavy." Norah commented.

"Well, we ran around the fields and the girls shrieked and hollered. The cows just looked at us like we were crazy and lumbered off. I got cow pies stuck on my best high heels and Ralph asked me why I never wanted to have any fun." Ros ground her teeth together at the thought of that argument. She wanted go get out of this town and go somewhere else. Somewhere she could be Rosalind and not plain Ros.

"Your face getting dark as a thundercloud. That lightening going strike any minute." Norah laughed sympathetically. "You just out with the wrong crowd, Sweetie. That's all. Here, have one of these to sweeten your disposition a little. I got a fresh cup of coffee for you right here. I'm popping some brownies in the oven for tomorrow. Be done in just a minute. Have some of them too. Your disposition sure could use it."

"The Hildebrands are coming tomorrow." Ros pursed her lips at the thought.

"She still bent on turning this into one of those fancy coffee houses with the bar-ista? Sounds like a terrorist to me. Bar-i-sta. But I'm just sayin'." Norah stirred milk into her frosting mix. "That woman think this town going come and buy whipped up coffees. These folk like their coffee bit-Ter and strong. They ain't going go for that latte stuff. Ain't no telling some folk though. I be out of a job. She want fancy stuff. Not fried pies and brownies and cobbler."

"She wants to spruce the place up. All cats and lace curtains and cloth napkins." Ros sniffed. Prices would go up with the fancy stuff and business would go down. And no Norah. No business. But the Hildebrands wouldn't listen when she talked about it with them. They were absentee owners, doing all their business over the phone. Had never even stepped in the Oak Corners Coffee Pot. Callie Hildebrand just wanted what she wanted. It didn't matter much. Ros was leaving anyway. Getting out of this trap of a town before she couldn't.

"Well. I tole that Ralph about this when he was in here. Tole him about me not having a job soon. He likes mah pies. Didn't sit well with him. Got no brains but he sure do eat. Good taste, that boy." Norah frosted a cupcake. "He sure do like my pies."

"Wish he liked something better than wild dates that don't go anywhere,' Ros groused.

"Like that time he took you down to the river to watch the sunset," Norah mused, eying a cupcake that needed a touch up on the frosting.

"And threw me in...great fun," Ros said sarcastically. She'd gone with Ralph since high school and he just never grew up. She loved him but he just never grew up.

"Wash them dishes and get ready to go. I got a couple of cakes to finish. Then we done."

"*Forever*," The silent plea wisped through Ros's head. "*Forever.*"

Ros opened the door promptly at 5 A.M. The sun streamed through the uncurtained windows. Three old farmers sat down at a table and ordered coffee. Their wives had made them coffee for years but now slept in. Since the farmers had never learned to make their own coffee, they were early morning regulars.

"Hot and black," Lindy, the day help, said as she sat their coffee down alongside a plate of toast and jam. The old men thanked her and began discussing the sorghum crop.

"Hildebrands are coming." Ros said.

"Well, they ain't here now," Lindy said heavily. "Nobody but Buddy, Bub, and Charlie. 'Spect Hank and Will to be here anytime to join 'em. Like old hens nesting and gossiping. And they say women are bad."

But the Hildebrands never came in. Folks came in and said, yes, they'd seen 'em. They were down by the river or touring the town, or out by the old stage stop. Somebody said they saw them at the Legion baseball game, eating hot dogs and drinking beer. Someone snickered something about snipe hunts later that night.

By 6:00 that evening, Ros just knew that Ralph was going to miss their date. They were supposed to go to Pickens to that nice new steakhouse on the highway. But Ralph, like the Hildebrands, never showed. How could a nice handyman like Ralph be so forgetful? This was the last straw. The very last straw. The straw that broke the camel's back straw. She was leaving this town and Ralph too. She sat the cup down heavily in front of Hank who finally arrived for dinner with Will. He gazed thoughtfully after her, wiping up the coffee spill with his napkin.

"What do ya think's a matter with her?" he asked Will.

"Ralph," Will said, putting sugar in coffee and stirring it.

"Probably. No brains, that boy." Hank sipped his coffee and winked at Will.

Norah came in to bake. Still no Hildebrands and Ralph had failed to call her.

"Uh-oh. Thundering up again in here," Norah said to Lindy. Lindy shrugged and poured Will and Hank more coffee. They all smiled, just watching and waiting.

Early the next morning Ros was really ticked off. Her bags were packed and her car was ready to go. She was just waiting for the Hildebrands so she could toss her resignation on the counter, flounce out and start her new life. She was going to go to New York City to see the Statue of Liberty and then get a job, any job, in Dallas, Texas. If Dallas wouldn't do, then she was going to Kansas City or Albuquerque or Denver or Seattle. Someplace big and grand. Maybe even Alaska. She had no idea what she would do but it was going to be something somewhere besides this diner and this town. But there were no Hildebrands to dramatically hand her resignation to so she just sat and waited and stewed.

The Hildebrands straggled in after church. They hadn't even gone to church and straggle was the operative word. They were covered in grass stains, and Callie had hay in her hair which looked like she hadn't brushed it in a week. Her husband, Gabe, looked tired but happy. They were much younger than Ros expected.

"You must be Ros. Oh, I'm so sorry we didn't come over right away yesterday. This is such a nice town. Everyone is just so nice. We got a tour and we've hit all the high spots," Callie gushed, shaking Ros' hand and holding it.

"Even went on a snipe hunt. Haven't done that since Boy Scouts," Gabe grinned. "And I played first base at the ball game. A lot of fun. This is a great town."

Callie moved past Ros. "You must be Lindy and oh, Norah. I hear you make the best pies. I can't wait to try one of your pies." She hugged Norah.

"Baby, I make 'em with love. Love, baby. That's what it takes." Norah hugged her and then handed her a plate of fried pies.

Callie and Gabe sat down eagerly in a booth. Gabe started and then rubbed his hip. "Guess we need to upgrade a little."

"New seats but not enough upgrade to change the charm of this place. People like tradition," Callie said as she took a bite of her fried peach pie. "Um. Cinnamon."

"That's what makes a pie good. That cinnamon, baby," Norah said, sitting down a cup of coffee.

"Well, Norah, I hope you stay here a long time cooking these because I intend to be here eating them,' Gabe said. "Wow. Excellent coffee. Hot and black. Like coffee should be."

"I really thought we could make this into a boutique coffee house but that's not going to work here. I like what you've done, Ros. Needs a little fixing but the food is wonderful and people are comfortable coming here. That's what makes a business." Callie said in between bites. "Now, Ralph said he was taking you over to Pickens. He says there is going to be a fancy brunch at the new steakhouse today. You take the afternoon off and go get ready," Callie added.

"Huh, I'm not falling for that again," Ros shrugged to herself. "More coffee, Callie?" she asked.

"Thanks. He's such a funny guy. Really showed us the town. We had such a lovely time and I understand how things here are much better. He really is a smart guy. You should hang on to that one," Callie urged.

Ralph came through the front door in a sports jacket and tie, all ready to take her to Pickens. "You ready? Sorry I didn't take you last night but I wanted to show the Hildebrands the town." Ralph looked pretty handsome. He cleaned up well. But......

"You could have at least called." Ros wasn't ready to reconsider leaving town and Ralph yet.

"Dressed up like that for you, Baby. Give him a chance." Norah whispered to Ros.

"Well, I guess I'll just go like I am," Ros said. "It doesn't matter anyway. We're never getting to Pickens." She sighed as she eyed his truck through the plate glass window.

"Honey, why not? He's here. Look at him. All dressed up like that. Course he's taking you to Pickens."

"Sure. Let's go, Ralph." Ros took his hand and they headed out to his pick-up. Everyone turned to watch them go. They walked out to the pick-up and Ros stopped.

"Ralph, why are there waders and fishing poles in your truck?" she asked sweetly.

"What? Oh, those. I, uh, just put them there in the back just in case, you know?" Ralph's hand on her lower back gently pushed her toward the passenger door. "Come on, let's go."

"In case of what? Ros planted her feet solidly, not moving. "We aren't really going to Pickens are we?"

"Course we are, I just thought, if we had time, we could drop a line in at the fishin' hole on the way home." He stammered a bit, and his ears turned red.

The brunch was actually nice, but the best part, according to Ros, was watching Ralph squirm in his jacket and tie. He was obviously uncomfortable in the fancy surroundings. He was kind of cute, she thought, with his ears still all red, and the sweat beading on his forehead. Ros smiled to herself, then shook her head. "*No, I am not giving in. I am not ready to forgive him.*" She failed to make eye contact with Ralph while she quietly firmed up her resolve to leave Oak Corners as soon as they got back to the coffee shop. Her car was waiting for her, all packed up. "*I'll tell him when he stops at the fishing hole on the way home.*"

Sure enough, Ralph slowed the truck down just before the turn-off to the fishing hole. Ros tensed up, knowing what was coming. She didn't want to hurt him, but she was determined to go through with it. She did not notice Ralph's hands shaking on the steering wheel, or see when he rubbed them, one at a time, on his pants.

She sat in the truck for a minute, steeling herself, after Ralph got out. The passenger door opened, startling her. She looked out at a smiling, pale Ralph. His hand was in his pocket.

"Ros, I know you like places like that steakhouse and, well, even if I did feel a bit like a fish out of water in there, if I promise to take you out like that at least once a month..." he got down on one knee, pulled his hand out of his pocket and extended it toward her. "Will you . . . um . . . will you marry me?"

Her eyes wide, she opened her mouth, but nothing would come out. She looked at Ralph's hand as is slowly opened up. There on his palm, was a . . . fishing lure! "What? Oh, I . . ."

"Ros?" He looked down at his hand, "Oops! Wrong pocket!"

As he reached for the other pocket, Ros jumped out of the truck, wrapped her arms around his neck and kissed him. "Yes. Yes! Of course I will marry you! That was the most perfect proposal! I will be able to tell our grandkids how you 'hooked' me with a fishing lure!"

www.ingramcontent.com/pod-product-compliance
Lightning Source LLC
Chambersburg PA
CBHW070555180626
46817CB00005B/1857